GERRY ANDERSON'S

GEMINI ● FORCE 1

GHOST MINE

Also by M. G. Harris

Gemini Force One: Black Horizon

GERRY ANDERSON'S

GHOST MINE
M. G. HARRIS

Orion
Children's Books

First published in Great Britain in 2015
by Orion Children's Books
an imprint of Hachette Children's Group
a division of Hodder and Stoughton Ltd
Carmelite House
50 Victoria Embankment
London EC4Y 0DZ
An Hachette UK company

1 3 5 7 9 10 8 6 4 2

A catalogue record for this book
is available from the British Library

ISBN 978 1 4440 1408 2

Typeset by Input Data Services Ltd, Bridgwater, Somerset

Printed and bound by CPI Group (UK) Ltd, Croydon, CR0 4YY

www.orionchildrensbooks.co.uk

For Josie, my first young reader,
still the biggest fan of my adventure stories.
− M. G. Harris

For my dad, who would have loved to see his
work excite and entertain a whole new generation.
− Jamie Anderson

How Gerry Anderson's
Gemini Force One Got off the Ground

An introduction from
Gerry's younger son Jamie

After completing work on what would be his final television series (*New Captain Scarlet*) my father – Gerry Anderson (creator of cult classics like *Fireball XL5*, *Thunderbirds* and *Space: 1999*) – began work on a new sci-fi adventure series. However, this time it wasn't a TV series or a film . . . it was a novel.

As he worked I could see something really thrilling emerging. Something with all the excitement and adventure you might expect from an episode of his most famous creation – *Thunderbirds* – combined with a more modern feel that he'd started to explore in his *New Captain Scarlet* series.

Sadly, it soon became apparent to us – and to him – that he was already living with Alzheimer's disease. And so, over time, his progress on the book slowed.

Eventually he was forced to stop work as his ability to read and write was taken from him. It seemed so cruel that a man who loved nothing more than to write and create was no longer able to do so. Even so – his desire to get this final project rolling stuck with him right up until the end.

Dad died on 26th December 2012.

In the days and weeks after Dad's funeral, I began to piece together the projects he'd been working on before he was forced to abandon them due to his dementia. I really felt there was something special in this final project, and started to explore the possibility of getting it completed.

Not too long after I'd started working on it, I met with M.G. Harris. She wrote a treatment of the first few chapters using material Dad had left behind. When I read it, things suddenly felt like they'd fallen into place. The content, the dialogue, the pace . . . it all felt so authentic. We had our author! We also finally decided on a name for the project – Gemini Force One.

We approached a number of publishers, but we couldn't seem to find one who would take the project without changing so many elements of the story that it no longer felt like a Gerry Anderson creation. So we turned to the crowdfunding website, Kickstarter.

After a month of planning, we launched the campaign. The response blew us away. Over 600 fans from all over the world put their own hard-earned cash into our project to make sure we could complete and publish the book in the way that Dad would have wanted.

And the good news didn't stop there – a short time later, we had a very exciting meeting with Orion. They loved the book and, best of all, they didn't want to change it! Very soon, we'd struck a deal to publish Gemini Force One!

I'm amazed that so much has happened in such a short time, and that we're now in a position to introduce Gemini Force One to new and existing Gerry Anderson fans all over the world. I'm incredibly grateful to those who have helped us make this happen – all of our wonderful Kickstarter backers, M.G. Harris, our agent Robert Kirby, and of course Amber and the team at Orion.

Stand by for action!

◤ ROCK SNAKES OF MARS ◥

The queue for tour T-shirts was insane; posters too. Someone had seriously underestimated how popular Rock Snakes of Mars would be. Ben Carrington was fairly certain that they hadn't been this sizzling hot six months ago, when he'd watched them perform at the Carrington Sky-High Hotel in Abu Dhabi.

'When did the Snakes go mainstream?' he murmured to Jasmine Dietz, who stood beside him in the line. 'Or is it just here? Bit odd – being huge in Switzerland, and nowhere else.'

The question seemed to amuse the fifteen-year-old daughter of Gemini Force's chief of operations. 'Duh! Rock Snakes are big news *everywhere*. That new album – *XLV*? It's number one in five countries. Their lead singer; Holden White? He's all over Youtube now, all over it.' She dimpled with a smile for him. 'A couple of months on GF One and you're already this much out of the loop?'

Ben just shrugged. He *could* have told Jasmine about the six a.m. starts, the hour of cardiac and weight training he did in the fitness room each morning, alongside Gemini Force crew members. He could have told her about the technical manuals he was studying, the flight simulators, and the chores he'd been assigned: cooking and laundry. He could have told her about the daily training sessions in the Israeli Defence Force's martial art, *krav maga*, or how their trainer, James Winch, had informed the crew that they had to 'get serious with this stuff'. Gemini Force was on the radar of at least one wanted villain – Minos Winter. It stood to reason other bad guys wouldn't be far behind.

'Jason Truby didn't plan for Gemini Force to be any kind of paramilitary group,' James had reasoned. 'But we have to be prepared to defend ourselves. Not every disaster is caused by an accident, or what the insurance companies like to call an 'act of God'. Minos Winter isn't the first guy that someone hired to create mayhem. He won't be the last, either.'

So – *krav maga*, every day.

Ben's muscles and bones had ached from the strain of it. He'd moved beyond grunts of pain as he took blows that got harder as he became stronger. Until one day he'd reacted with lightning speed – two swift defensive kicks in succession and a drop-roll.

James Winch had rewarded him with a tight smile. 'Muscle memory,' he'd said. 'Finally!'

Ben *could* have told Jasmine about all of this. But he just sucked in a breath of ice-cold air and gave her a wry grin. 'I've been kind of busy.'

It had been almost two months since Ben had last seen her. When Michael Dietz had invited him and Rigel back to Switzerland for a few days at the end of the year, the thought of seeing Jasmine had been part of the attraction. Ben kind of missed hanging around with someone closer to his own age.

'Life on GF One. I'm enjoying it,' Ben said. 'But don't get me wrong – it's no picnic.'

Jasmine punched him gently in the left arm. 'That's what you were looking for though, yes? Something *intense*. To take your mind off your mother's death.'

'If you say so,' Ben said, with a slight shake of his head.

But he didn't deny it.

At first, Ben had found Jasmine's bluntness a little hard to take. He wasn't used to being around girls all that much and hadn't met anyone quite like her.

With no sisters and spending most of the past six years in boys-only boarding schools, girls were a bit of a mystery. His old school had organised mixers with girls from nearby schools, but the weird way girls behaved at those events had put him off trying to get a girlfriend.

'Pity there isn't a manual that can explain girls,' he mused, half to himself.

Jasmine turned to him with an enigmatic smile. 'Oh, but there are. Lots. We're very easy to understand.'

'So, your boyfriend, does he understand you?' Ben leaned against the brick wall, his freezing fingers stuffed in the pockets of his North Face windcheater jacket. He'd been in the subtropical climes of GF One's Caribbean location for long enough that he'd forgotten how to dress for an alpine winter. Gloves would have been a good move tonight.

'Jonah?' she said. 'Obviously not – or I wouldn't be at a concert with another boy.'

'Oh,' said Ben, keeping his voice deliberately flat. 'I see.' He turned away, pretending to peer at the merchandise booth. He was surprised to hear from her own lips that Jasmine wasn't a *thousand* per cent into Jonah. Even more surprising was the warm feeling it gave him to hear it. They were only five customers away from the front of the line. The Rock Snakes' show had finished almost an hour ago, but there were still hundreds of fans around. 'Think I'm going to get a few shirts for the guys back on GF One. They'll get a kick out of us all wearing the same.'

She eyed him quizzically. 'Why? They're all in uniform anyway.'

Ben puffed a cloud of freezing breath up into the fringe of his light–brown hair. 'Not me.'

It was a tiny bone of contention between Ben and Jason Truby, the founder and leader of Gemini Force. Although Truby had agreed to let Ben spend time on the base during a year off before he started sixth form, he hadn't agreed to let Ben become fully part of the team.

Ben trained with them, went on drills and exercises, had even been allowed to assist in a couple of minor rescues. But he hadn't yet pulled on the anthracite-grey uniform of Gemini Force, made entirely from a customised Kevlar fabric.

Maybe it was just a symbol. But symbols mattered.

Ten minutes later they left the arena in Bern, with drawstring and tote bags stuffed with T-shirts, key rings and plush black-and-red snakes with beady, plastic green eyes – the band's mascot, Dylan.

Michael Dietz's home was dark when Ben and Jasmine arrived. The apartment was situated on the edge of the city near the river Aare, in a south-eastern suburb of Bern. Ben and Jasmine found Rigel waiting eagerly, tail wagging his whole body. In his jaws, the dog picked up his lead from where it lay on the floor of the spacious entrance hall. With hopeful eyes, he presented it to Ben.

'Yucky dog-spit,' Ben said cheerfully, rubbing the head and ears of his flat-coated retriever. 'Hope you haven't been eating any dog poop, old boy.'

Jasmine wrinkled her nose and said in a lowered voice, 'He does that? Gross!'

Ben grinned. 'Ha, no! Not any more. But he used to. Pups do that.' He fastened the metal clip to Rigel's collar. 'Can you tell Dietz I'm going to take him for a walk?'

She looked surprised. 'This late? It's so cold.'

Jasmine's father, Michael Dietz, appeared in the doorway to the living room. He was barefoot, dressed in pyjama bottoms and a long-sleeved T-shirt. His thick, greying hair was still gelled into a slightly unruly pompadour, so he probably hadn't yet gone to bed.

'No need,' he said, with a nod towards Rigel. 'I already took him. Ben's doggy is trying to take advantage of his master's good nature. Now you kids need to come inside and talk.' Dietz looked at Ben, his eyes serious. 'Jason Truby has been in touch.'

They went into the darkened living room and settled onto the couch opposite the windows. Outside, Ben could see the pale reflection of an almost full moon on distant mountain peaks.

Dietz switched on a single lamp and took a seat near the teenagers. 'Jason wants you to do some mountain training.'

Ben nodded. 'Yeah, that's part of why I'm here. It's been ages since Rigel did anything at altitude. I want to spend a couple of days with him – camping, maybe a bit of climbing, laying some trails for him. All of that.'

'Jason thinks it wouldn't be a bad idea for some of the Gemini Force guys to join you. They could use the altitude training too.' Dietz turned to Jasmine. 'You might be interested as well. He wants you all to heli up above the snow line. There could even be some skiing.'

Jasmine gave a little shrug of her shoulders. 'Sure. Always fun to start the ski season early.'

'I bet you ski pretty well,' Ben said, approvingly. He'd never met a Swiss who didn't.

'Jasmine was offered a trial for the Olympic squad,' Dietz said, with a touch of pride.

Ben stared. 'Serious?'

She laughed. 'They might have been. But I wasn't. I won some junior medals for ski cross, so what? I didn't want to compete. Athletes have no lives outside of sport.'

'Ski cross?' Ben said. 'Epic! Still, nice to be asked, right? I mean, I'm OK on skis, but you wouldn't get me doing those crazy stunts.'

'I'll tell Jason yes, shall I?' Dietz said.

Ben and Jasmine shared a smile.

'I guess,' said Ben. 'I mean, it's probably an order, isn't it?'

Dietz shook his head, slowly. It could have been Ben's imagination but he fancied that he glimpsed a crafty grin twitching at the edges of Dietz's mouth. 'What you do as a result of your association with Gemini Force must be of your own free will, Ben. This could involve some physical challenges that you'll find rather taxing.'

'Sounds like a laugh,' Ben said. 'I'm up for anything! I was born and raised in the mountains, Dietz. Born and raised.'

'All right then,' said Dietz. The crafty smile intensified. 'Get some sleep. You'll need it.'

━ LIGHTNING START ━

He felt a hand gripping his shoulder, shaking him awake. In his ear, a harsh whisper.

'Lightning start. We leave in five.' By the time Ben turned his face towards the voice, whoever had woken him had gone.

Ben had become accustomed to fast starts, straight from bed. It was part of the training at GF One. Since each member of the team shifted their personal clock by an hour each day on a staggered timetable, someone was always dragged out of bed for the lightning starts.

'Disasters have no timetable. Gemini Force isn't the fire service. We aren't the police. Paramedics go home to their ordinary lives. But that's not us,' Truby had told Ben. 'With us, it's a full-time job. And that means twenty-four-seven.'

Ben was dressed and had joined Dietz and Rigel in the kitchen within four minutes. He didn't bother with washing on lightning starts. You got pretty sweaty doing rescue work anyway – he didn't see the point of wasting precious time just to start the day smelling like soap.

Rubbing his eyes with the back of one hand, he gave Rigel an absent-minded pat with the other. The dog responded only with a soft whine as he crunched breakfast – a carefully measured serving of dry dog food. Ben reached for two pieces of the peanut butter on toast that Dietz was heaping onto a plate.

Jasmine arrived three minutes later. Like Ben, she'd dressed for the mountains; hiking trousers, a figure-hugging cream microfleece, mahogany leather climbing boots. Her long brown hair was neatly brushed away from her face, her hazel eyes were bright and lively. When she sat next to him he caught the whiff of honey and vanilla. 'You washed,' he said, and smiled. 'Classic noob manoeuvre.'

'Are you kidding? I'd have to be in a burning building before I'd leave the house without at least a wash.'

'That's kind of the point,' Ben said. He passed Jasmine the plate, watched her take one triangular piece of toast. 'The people we're trying to save might be.'

'Rather you than me,' she said. 'Don't get me wrong, I like to visit. But Gemini Force isn't my idea of a career. I prefer something more creative.'

'Still, I bet there's loads you could do on GF One,' began Ben, but he caught sight of Dietz shaking his head. Behind his daughter, Dietz raised a single finger to his lips and smiled.

Ben heard the sound of lift doors sliding open. Each apartment had access to the building's storage rooms. There were footsteps in the entrance hall. Someone was carrying something back and forth to the lift, Ben concluded.

'Who else is here?' he asked Dietz.

'Eat,' Dietz advised. He handed them each a sealed bottle of spring water, plus an extra one for Ben. 'For Rigel.'

Jasmine stood. 'I'll fetch my day-hiking pack.'

Dietz shook his head. 'Nope. This time you go empty-handed. Apart from water.'

Addison Nicole Dyer, Gemini Force's newest pilot, strolled into the kitchen. She was dressed in thermal trousers and a winter-weight hiking jacket and boots. Her dark brown, sleekly bobbed hair matched the chocolate colour of her jacket.

She clapped gloved hands together, 'Dudes, let's go. From this moment, consider this a training mission. Paul Scott is the superior crew member so he's *el capitano*. If you wanna withdraw at this point, OK. Once we're on the mountain, you're going to need to follow orders. It can turn pretty life-or-death up there. As you should both know.'

A mobile phone buzzed twice. Addison reached into her pocket, reacting to what she saw onscreen with a wry grin.

'Scuzzball,' she announced.

Ben said, 'Pardon?'

'The go-word. Truby's changed it to *scuzzball*. As of now.'

Jasmine turned to Ben. 'Go-word?'

'It's like, a code,' he said. 'If one of us says it, it means trouble. It means, *"get the heck out of Dodge, without a glance at what you leave behind".*'

'And you're supposed to just go?'

Ben nodded. 'It's not meant to be used unless you're pretty sure you're going to die, and the rest of the team is at risk.'

Jasmine frowned. 'Wow. I'm kind of glad my dad gets to stay on GF One, if it's like that.'

'Oh, hardly ever,' Addison said, lightly. Rigel approached the pilot with the suppressed eagerness of a well-trained but delighted dog. 'Hey, boy,' she said, rubbing him behind the left ear. 'You wanna come ride in a heli?' She glanced at Ben and Jasmine expectantly. 'Good to go?'

As one, Ben and Jasmine rose to their feet.

'GTG,' said Ben.

The adrenaline was beginning to flow quite nicely. He wasn't quite sure what Paul and Addison had planned, but they were managing to inject a bit of drama into the mission, which he appreciated. It couldn't match the pure adrenaline spikes you got when things *really* started to happen, but still.

It was a short drive through the deserted early morning streets, out of Bern and onto the highway towards the small town of Belp. Soon enough they'd reached the small Bern–Belp airport and were driving towards the private charter section, where Ben could already see the waiting Robinson R44 helicopter. He felt a stab of sorrow as he looked at the helicopter that his mother had once purchased for her own start-up rescue agency, the Caroliners.

There was no point thinking about it. But once in a while Ben couldn't help but remember that if the Caroliners hadn't gone bust along with every other business owned by the Carringtons, then maybe his mother would still be alive.

Fate had chosen a different path for his mother, and for him. Now his life was physically and mentally more gruelling than he'd imagined was possible without actually being in the armed forces. He rarely complained though. Every time he got hurt in training, every time he felt too tired to do a lightning start, every time he found it hard to fall asleep at midday because his internal clock had wound twelve hours ahead, Ben just swallowed each negative thought.

Truby had given Ben an amazing opportunity, letting him spend a year on GF One. He wasn't about to ruin that by whining; that was the first important thing. And – the second? Jasmine was right. Life on GF One left Ben with no energy to feel sorry for himself about losing his parents and the family fortune.

Which was just how he wanted it.

He took his place in the rear of the R44, sliding in next to Rigel and Jasmine. He'd offered to help Paul load four medium-sized rucksacks into the luggage compartment. The Australian pilot had politely but firmly refused. Ben couldn't stop a nagging feeling that Paul was keen to take absolute control of the training mission, even deciding exactly what equipment they should each take. Paul hadn't even consulted him on what to bring for Rigel. Pretty vexing.

Ben himself wouldn't have done it that way. Surely getting suitably equipped was part of the job? If he ever organised a mountain survival session, Ben would make their *first* task the selection of appropriate kit.

The R44 was up in the air and flying below a high bank of thick white cloud. Straight ahead to the south of the city, the line of peaks in the Bernese Alps was just visible. Only the summits of the Mönch and the Jungfrau were shrouded in mist.

Ben sunk his fingers into the thick, soft black fur at the base of Rigel's neck. He massaged the dog's muscles as Rigel bent his head and nuzzled affectionately against Ben's thigh. It was really *very* odd that no one had thought to ask Ben about what equipment he'd need for Rigel. The dog's training was Ben's responsibility, no one else's. He ought to have been given time to put together a training plan.

'So, guys,' he said loud enough to be heard in the front, over the clatter of the rotor blades. 'What's the plan? I was hoping to be able to get in some specific training for Rigel. It'd be great if I could get a heads-up, y'know. Help me to think up some stuff to do with him.'

'Don't you worry about that,' replied Paul. 'We'll talk about all that tomorrow. Today is just for getting in some skiing on fresh, fresh powder. And some obligatory après-ski.'

Paul's response wasn't quite what Ben had hoped for. Sure, he wanted to have fun. It had been months since he'd skied. Memories of the previous season came flooding back. St Anton with his mother at Christmas and again in February, Mount Cook in New Zealand with both parents in July – just a week before his father's death in the Annapurna region of the Himalayas.

But they only had a few days to spare. Time that would be more usefully spent training.

'You don't seem too excited,' Jasmine observed. 'I guess heli-skiing is no big deal to you? But I've never done it.'

'Me too,' called out Paul.

'Me three,' said Addison, leaning back for a second to smirk at Ben. 'Never even been on skis. So don't *you* be the buzz-kill.'

'I *am* excited,' Ben objected, and stopped there. No one was actually saying it, but he was getting a faint vibe from them. Like he was some spoiled rich kid who was trying hard to appear blasé.

They all fell silent as Addison piloted the helicopter over the looming Eiger North Wall, towards the craggy rock and ice of the shark-tooth-shaped Schreckhorn.

Paul turned to face Ben and Jasmine. 'We're headed for the Bernese Oberland glaciers. Addi's going to drop us off near the high altitude ski hut, where we've ordered ski equipment, maps and a sledge for Rigel. We'll take our kit, ski to where the snow ends, to our mountain hut. Finding it – that's the first task. Next, we'll hike down into the valley, find the nearest village. Grab a ride home. Pretty straightforward bit of skiing and hiking. Shouldn't be out longer than two nights. And tomorrow, Ben, on the way down to the valley, you can do some trail work with Rigel.'

Ben had to admit, it was a great-sounding plan. He settled back into his seat, one hand still on Rigel's throat. Life on GF One could get pretty intense. Maybe he just needed to remember how to *chill*.

⟋ GONE ⟍

'That's the best powder I've ever skied on. And the views – amazing!'

Paul Scott nodded his vigorous agreement with Jasmine's comment, delivered over a mug of steaming cocoa. They'd made such good time that Paul had suggested they passed up spending the night at the luxurious climbers' lodge en route, and continued to a genuine mountain hut. 'We can reach it in about an hour, if we go fast. Then, Ben, if you're so keen to do some work with Rigel, you'll have more time.'

You couldn't accuse the mountain hut of luxury; but then again, this trip wasn't just for pleasure.

The views today had been impressive, but with the sky a blanket of low cloud, it wasn't all that obvious where the mountains ended and the sky began. Ben had enjoyed far more spectacular days of heli-skiing with his parents, but he kept that to himself. Paul and Jasmine had never done this before. There was something exhilarating about experiencing anything together when it was someone's first time. He wasn't going to spoil that for any of the group.

Ben had insisted on pulling Rigel's sled himself. Paul and Jasmine had offered to take a turn, but he had refused. He might be on his own with the dog one day, in a life-threatening situation. He had to know he could manage alone. Several times, Paul and Jasmine had paused, waiting for Ben and Rigel to catch up. Then they'd set off again without giving Ben a chance to rest. He'd arrived at the hut out of breath, his undershirt damp with sweat, in spite of the biting cold.

The mountain hut had taken some finding. It had once been a cattle shelter. The building conversion hadn't managed to get the acrid stink of silage out of the wood in that half of the hut. There was only one bedroom, with four double bunks. The bathroom had hot running water and a chemical toilet. It was on the smelly side of the house. The living area was equipped with a wood-burning stove. An assortment of stainless steel pots and pans hung from sturdy hooks in the low ceiling.

Once they'd arrived and put their ski equipment in the boot cupboard to dry out, they'd set about unpacking the rucksacks that Paul had prepared. Ben was relieved to see that everything he could think of was there – Rigel's wearable computer technology collar, walkie-talkies, a harness for carrying the dog, an assortment of climbing gear, a GPS locator, an emergency survival kit.

The pack that had come down the slopes next to Rigel on the sled was filled with food and drink. Ben had taken the milk and a generous wedge of local mountain cheese. He'd found a dry, empty insulated box under the low rough pine table in the living area. He'd packed it with snow and placed the milk and cheese inside. The rest of the supplies, pasta, pellets of dog food, plastic containers of sauce, a hunk of German salami, a loaf of sliced bread, cereal bars, chocolate bars and apples, he'd put on the square of kitchen sideboard next to the stove.

Paul had cooked for them – pasta with salami and cheese. They'd leaned back onto the hard cushions of the bench sofa and raised mugs of cocoa to a great day on the mountain.

Rigel had crouched at Ben's feet, a towel draped around him. On the way down, the dog had taken to the snow every so often, bounding along beside Ben and the sledge, until he'd tired from the effort. The dry powder that had caked around his body had begun to melt. An aroma of damp dog fur slowly encircled them.

After the exhausting day, sleep had descended with surprising, almost overwhelming speed.

Ben was usually a light sleeper, but he woke to find the cold glare of white light in his face. It streamed relentlessly through the thin curtains. He took several minutes to stir. Puzzled, he sat up. He checked his watch. How could it already be ten o'clock?

In the bunk opposite, Jasmine was still fast asleep, cosy inside her mummy-shaped sleeping bag. On Paul's bunk, a crumpled sleeping bag lay empty. The black towel that Rigel had slept on lay in a heap on the pinewood floor.

Ben stood up. He felt unsteady, still half-asleep. Maybe it was the relentless physical exercise of the previous day? Even so, it was unusual for his body to be so reluctant to recover. As soon as he emerged from his sleeping bag, Ben wrapped his arms around his chest, tucked both hands under his arms. It was cold enough to see his breath.

He glanced at the bathroom. Its door was slightly ajar; the room was empty. He listened for a moment. The hut was silent. An ominous feeling began to stir within him. Ben stepped into the living area. This was his first real shock.

Two backpacks were open, partially inside-out, apparently discarded at the corners of the room. The contents – mainly clothes – had been strewn randomly around the room. Of the other two backpacks, there was no sign. He checked the kitchen sideboard. What was left of the food they'd brought was gone.

Ben drew a deep, shaky breath. It was so quiet that he could still hear the faint sound of Jasmine stirring in the bedroom. He went to the front door, opened it. It hadn't been locked, which was pretty normal in the mountains, in Ben's experience – even in villages. Outside, the snow was like a smooth white river that flowed from the front door, continued down the slope for about a hundred metres, and then petered out.

And the cold! Within seconds he could feel heat being sucked out of him, leaving his body through the exposed skin of his face and hands. His cheeks twitched at the bite of it. His eyeballs seemed suddenly dry, like stones. Teeth chattering, Ben closed the front door to the hut.

He stood absolutely still, listening. Nothing, not even the sound of birds, since the trees only began a hundred metres away. Quieter even than yesterday, when most of the time there'd been nothing but the swish and shuss of their own skis on the virgin powder.

Slowly, Ben went back into the hut, closed the door firmly behind him. He went to the wood-burning stove in the corner. A brushed-steel chimney reached into the ceiling. He warmed his hands for a few moments on the stove. He took one of the remaining five wedges of wood from the neatly arranged heap by the stove, and fed it into the dying fire.

Then he went back into the bedroom. As gently as he could, he woke Jasmine. She seemed groggy too. Yawning, she joined him on the sofa. 'Where's Paul?'

'Something's happened.'

'What d'you mean?'

Ben gathered up a few pieces of clothing from what had been scattered around. 'Paul's gone. He's taken the food, all the equipment. And Rigel.'

'Paul's left us?'

'Looks like it.'

Jasmine seemed doubtful. 'I can't believe we didn't hear him.'

'Yeah well, I don't normally sleep from nine-thirty till ten the next morning.'

She glanced at him. 'You think he gave us something?'

'Slipped us a Mickey Finn? Yup, I do.'

'What about Rigel?'

Ben considered. 'Must have given him something, too. Rigel wouldn't have left without a fuss.' He picked up his hiking boots. 'D'you want to get changed in the bedroom? I'll change in here.'

Once he was dressed, Ben checked more thoroughly. This had to be some kind of test. But as he realised just how comprehensively they'd been cleaned out, his pulse rate began to climb.

The only thing he found was a climbing harness. Without it, there was no way to get Rigel down some of the sheer drops they'd surely face on the descent into the valley. He tried not to think through the implications of this and focused instead on the available food. To his relief, the ice box was closed, apparently forgotten. Floating in the snow-melt was about half a litre of milk and most of the cheese.

Jasmine returned wearing full hiking gear. With a rueful expression she held out a large bar of Cailler milk chocolate. 'I always keep some in my jacket when I'm in the mountains. I've also got lip balm, aspirin, gum and weirdly enough, dental floss.'

Ben reached for his North Face jacket, which lay in a pile on the floor. As he picked it up, he saw the edge of a red plastic box about thirty centimetres long, marked with the Swiss flag.

'The emergency kit!' With relief, Ben tucked it into one of his inner jacket pockets. He searched through everything one last time. Nothing else turned up.

'No sign of the map,' he said, dismally. 'I guess that's part of the test.'

He stood up. So – it was to be a survival hike; minimal supplies, no communication devices, in the freezing cold. A race against the clock; life or death stuff.

Because the *one* thing you did not want to risk in December was to be caught out at night.

➤ TRACKS ➤

'You think this is a test . . . ?' Jasmine seemed uncertain.

Ben was pretty confident. 'Are you kidding? Yeah, it's a survival test. Paul will have skied off on his own somewhere, he'll probably get himself and Rigel picked up by Addison not far from here.'

'But Paul's skis are still here,' she pointed out.

Ben hesitated. He hadn't checked the boot room yet. But when he pushed the wooden door open, there they were, along with his own skis, Jasmine's and the sled.

'Ah,' he said. '*Very* interesting.' He zipped up his jacket, tugged on his gloves, and pulled an electric-blue, thermal beanie hat over his head until it had covered his ears. A moment later, he was outside.

It took only a few seconds to find three sets of footprints leading away from the hut. Carefully, Ben inserted his own boot into each type of print.

'Three blokes,' he informed Jasmine, who had just joined him. 'Or very heavy women with massive feet.'

'No dog,' observed Jasmine. She seemed to be ignoring his quip.

Ben examined the dog tracks more carefully. She was right. They meandered, but you couldn't trace a complete, fresh set of prints from the house, only a set that came from yesterday's ski tracks.

'Damn,' he said softly. 'Someone must have carried Rigel out.'

'And we didn't hear anything?'

He shook his head. This was starting to get a little alarming. 'These are Paul's prints,' Jasmine said. There was a slight tremor in her voice. When Ben looked closely at the footprints, he could see why. In places, both feet dragged. As though Paul had been sliding.

'Looks like he was dragged,' Ben said, eventually. He followed the prints for about twenty metres before kneeling down. There were drops of blood in the snow. Not much, but enough.

For several moments, neither one said anything. Ben knew from experience just how mind-bogglingly unlikely it was to be attacked in the rural Alps. Never mind in such a remote location.

If Paul hadn't stolen away in the middle of the night as part of some kind of training exercise or prank, then the only other possibility was utterly chilling.

Someone had intentionally targeted Paul. Whoever it was had probably removed Rigel to prevent him from waking the others. They'd left Ben and Jasmine alone, with no means of communication and no food.

'Why did they leave us?' Jasmine said. It was obviously what they were both thinking.

'I don't think they wanted to harm us,' Ben said. 'But then again, I doubt that they care one way or the other.'

'What should we do?'

Ben considered for a few seconds. 'GF One knows we're here. But they're not expecting us until the day after tomorrow. That'd be the earliest that they'd send anyone to find out what happened.'

'If we stay, we'll freeze,' Jasmine said, with an involuntary shiver. 'There's not much firewood left. And we haven't got anything to chop trees with.'

'If we go,' he said, 'we can get to a village *today*. We can raise the alarm. The sooner they get on to whoever took Paul and Rigel, the better.'

'You think we can get there today?'

'I did see the map,' Ben said, thoughtfully. 'It's about ten klicks to the nearest village. But if we head south, we should eventually hit a road. I think the road was only eight kilometres away, as the crow flies. That's our quickest way out; hit the road, hitch a ride.'

'You think we can do that before dark?'

He nodded, at first tentative, then reassuring. 'Yes . . . I'm sure we can. But we need to get moving. It's already after ten. Let's get everything that might be useful into those two rucksacks and hit the trail.'

They gathered up the sleeping bags, wrapped them around the remaining pieces of firewood. They stuffed them into the rucksacks along with the climbing harness, survival kit and the lighter, which Ben found under the stove. They shared the remaining milk and cheese and set off, still chewing.

Fifty metres away, the footprint trail stopped, next

to snowmobile tracks, which headed west towards the wooded area that remained above the snow line.

'Now we know how they got to us without being heard,' Ben said. 'They didn't use a heli.' He broke off suddenly at the faint sound of a dog barking, somewhere in the woods.

'Rigel!' he shouted. 'RIGEL, RIGEL, RIGEL!'

He and Jasmine stared at each other in wonder and relief when a few seconds later, a bark echoed faintly in the distance.

It was impossible to tell how far away the dog was – in the silence of their Alpine surroundings, sound might travel a long way. After a minute, Ben couldn't wait. He started to follow the snowmobile tracks towards the woods. But before he reached the trees, Rigel's bounding black form shot out of the woodland, heading directly for Ben.

Rigel practically flew, skimming across the snow towards Ben. When he reached him, the collision almost knocked Ben off his feet. He bent to hug Rigel, trying to contain sixty kilos of energetic joy in his arms. The dog was beside himself with delight. But beneath his fur, Ben detected a steady tremble.

Rigel rubbed his nose against Ben's face. It was icy, icy cold. When he felt this, Ben wrapped both arms tightly around the dog, rubbing a gloved hand vigorously across his back. Jasmine caught up with them. Ben urged her to join in. They rubbed and cuddled the dog for at least five minutes, until Ben said, 'He's not shaking so much now. That was a close one, wasn't it, boy?'

He eyed the woods from where the dog had emerged, trying to work out how long the dog had been out in the open. Had he fallen off the snowmobile, been pushed? 'Or did you escape?' he wondered, looking into Rigel's eyes.

The dog pulled away, whining. He began to bound happily in the snow – leading back towards the woods. Ben took a step. 'What's in there, Rigel?'

Rigel didn't bark, but bounded a little further away, his tail wagging. He gave a low whine. It was obvious that he wanted to be followed.

'What's that, boy, trouble at the old mill?' Ben said, with a grin.

Jasmine asked, 'What makes you think there's a mill?'

'It's . . . I don't,' Ben said. 'It's a joke.'

'A joke,' she said, barely reacting. 'I'm sorry, I can't stop thinking about Paul. What do you think's happened?'

'Hey,' Ben said, firmly. 'Don't worry about Paul.' It was hard enough to keep his own thoughts from straying to dark places. 'We need to focus. Our job, Jazz, is to get out of here.'

Before we turn into a pair of ice lollies.

'Whatever's in that wood, Rigel wants us to go.'

'I agree.' Ben glanced back at the hut and the descent to the distant valley. It seemed more or less straightforward, until the slope hit some sheer cliff faces in the distance.

He assumed there was a route through the three vaguely conical peaks that rose from the ground, stopping very well short of the nearest rocky summit. But if there wasn't, it would be a risky strategy. The woodland, on the other hand, went west as far as the eye could see, always more or less at the same elevation.

He should have made Paul discuss the route last night. But they'd all been so tired, it hadn't occurred to him.

Rigel was well ahead of them now, almost at the woods. Ben hesitated for another second. Jasmine's quietness was beginning to worry him. It struck him that she might not be a confident hiker, even though she was Swiss.

'How're you feeling?' he said, reaching for her arm.

'I'm fine.' But she wouldn't meet his gaze.

'Fitness levels, energy?'

She nodded, vaguely. 'OK.'

'You ever hiked in winter before?'

Jasmine hesitated, her brow furrowed under the rim of her raspberry-coloured cable-knit beanie.

That's a no, he guessed.

Ben offered a hand. 'It's going to be all right. We've got some calories inside us. We've got your chocolate. We can make a fire. We just need to keep moving. And most of all – we've got Rigel. We'll get to the road before dark, Jazz, I promise you.'

Jasmine nodded, managed a timid smile.

A cold realisation came to Ben slowly. Jasmine was *scared*. She'd never been in a situation like this. Ben was the one with stamina and experience. It was up to him to see they all got home safely. And then . . . then they'd face up to the truth about Paul – whatever it was.

He made himself grin confidently, gave her hand a squeeze. 'Let's go. By the left . . . yeah! You've got it. Want to sing? I know some marching songs. No?' Ben shrugged. 'Fair enough.'

He held her hand tightly as they entered the woods.

━ LEAD ME ━

Rigel stayed ahead as they made their way through the trees. There was no path, but the trees were far apart on the slope. The snow was shallower than outside the wood – no more than five centimetres in places.

The fir trees, however, were heavily laden. Every so often the sheer weight of the snow would cause a block to slide from branches high up. Then there'd be a sound that had made them stop dead, the first time they'd heard it.

After an hour they hadn't made nearly as much progress as Ben had hoped. He made sure not to say anything. There was still no clue as to why Rigel had led them into the wood. The dog seemed to know where he was going, always ahead of them, occasionally looking to see that they were still following. He seemed happy. As though the three of them were on a long, juicy walk.

Yet Ben couldn't see anything but trees ahead. He was starting to have doubts. In an hour or two, he'd have to make a decision. Did they go back, return to the hut where at least they'd be warmer? Or keep going with no indication that this was the right way?

The sooner they got to a village, the sooner they could raise the alarm about Paul.

Ahead, they heard Rigel barking. Ben quickened his pace, relieved to see that Jasmine followed without comment. They needed to press on faster. He'd been working hard to maintain the illusion that they were out for a stroll, but now the silences between the two of them were growing longer. Neither dared to say it, but Ben was pretty sure that like him, Jasmine was thinking about Paul.

Rigel had found a waterfall. It was mostly frozen, thick, solid icicles like ripples at the edges giving way to a trickle of water in the centre. Ben glanced at the river bank on the way down the slope. It was mostly lined with low, wiry shrubs. They'd be safe handholds on the way down.

'We're going to follow this stream,' he said. 'It'll be the fastest, safest way down. Grab some of the undergrowth; wrap it around your hands. Stay away from the ice.'

They began to descend. It was slow, tiring work, with the snow concealing roots that occasionally tripped them. But he was right; the bare, scrubby bushes – Ben guessed they were bilberries – helped them to cling on as they made the steep descent. By noon they'd reached a ravine, facing a shallow, fast-flowing clear grey-green river, about three metres wide.

Ben looked both ways. He'd seen plenty of rivers like this in Austria. 'It's not very deep now, but look,' he said, pointing to smooth, ice-coated rocks about a metre off the river bank. 'It goes a lot higher. There's probably a hydroelectric plant somewhere upstream. They'll control the flow.'

'So we shouldn't wade across?'

He shook his head. 'No. Keep Rigel away too. When the cycle starts up again, the water level will go up in seconds. Get washed away in that and . . .' Ben drew a slow line across his throat. It would be a cold, terrifying death, to be swept away in that water. Happened all the time in the mountains, too; often when someone went in after a beloved pet.

Ben had a quick look at the stones and trees, checking on which side moss grew more thickly. 'North is that way,' he said, pointing somewhere behind them. 'The river's bending south-west.' He turned to face right, putting the riverbank on his left. 'We'll follow it down.'

Jasmine, however, had an odd look on her face. She kept glancing back the way they'd come.

'Did you hear something?' she asked.

'Like what?'

'Like . . . I don't know. Noises. From the woods.'

'Snow falling from the trees,' he said, sounding more confident than he was that there hadn't been anything else. But she was right. Ben hadn't wanted to admit it to himself, but there'd been a strange sensation as they'd slipped and scrambled down the slope. Once, he could have sworn he'd heard a voice. When he'd stopped, Rigel had looked at him and barked. As if to say, 'What's the hold-up?'

They walked for another hour, only pausing to break off pieces from Jasmine's bar of Cailler chocolate to share. In the far distance directly ahead, rocky walls rose behind the dark fringe of trees that had mostly lost their snow. They were headed straight for that rock face. The closer they got, the more Ben began to dread what they'd find. He checked his watch every few minutes, always when Jasmine had her back turned. It would be dark within four hours. And still absolutely no sign of civilisation.

Another worrying development that Ben hadn't reported was the fact that Rigel was no longer leading them. He wasn't sure how obvious it was, or whether Jasmine had noticed. There were things he'd learned about the dog's behaviour, subtle indicators that gave it away. Instead of trotting with his head and tail up and moving purposefully, he now took time to sniff around areas on the way, his head and tail down as he wandered at their side.

They were relying on Ben's hiking experience now.

The craggy rock face loomed closer until it seemed to actually lean over them, casting a shadow as they followed the river, winding its way through the ravine. The stream of water continued relentlessly. No wall of rock was going to impede its movement towards the nearest lake, or maybe even the River Aare itself.

Ben stopped. Jasmine had fallen behind. Without realising it, he'd ploughed on ahead, always speeding up, increasingly eager to discover that he'd made the right decision in coming this way. Rigel had been with her last time he'd checked. Now though, the dog was nowhere to be seen.

'Rigel?'

She shrugged, looked around. 'Isn't he with you?'

Ben stared into the trees, back up the slope. 'Rigel!' he roared. He didn't bother to disguise his anger. 'Come on, boy. I know you want to play. But we're not mucking around, here!'

From deep inside the woods, there was a short bark. Ben listened until he could hear the rustle of shifting snow as the dog leaped and bounded back to his master. When Rigel returned, Ben didn't touch him. Instead, he pointed sternly at the rock face. 'What the hell is that, hey? How are we supposed to get through it?'

Rigel whined a little, picking up on Ben's angry tone. He tried wagging his tail, but not very convincingly. Then he began to run towards the mountain wall. A few moments later, he was out of sight.

'Rigel!' called Ben. 'FIND! FIND! FIND!'

Jasmine finally caught up again. She was panting slightly. Ben wasn't surprised – the pace he was setting was tough. But if she didn't keep up . . . ? He couldn't allow that thought. The adrenaline flowed freely now. All his senses were heightened. He'd accepted that they were in danger, finally. This was survival mode.

But Ben wasn't ready to share that knowledge.

'What's he doing?'

'That's the command to find survivors. If there's a way through the mountain, Rigel will find it. Switzerland isn't a big country – someone is bound to have hiked here before. There'll be a scent trail.'

'What if it leads to a dead body?' Jasmine asked. Her face was pale, despite the exertion.

'It won't,' Ben said, grimly determined. He began to stride towards the rock wall.

Stay positive.

After ten minutes, he found Rigel waiting patiently by a narrow opening in the rock face. It was easily large enough for two full-grown men to enter, standing abreast. Ben turned, watching Jasmine making her way towards them. He approached the trees, examining the crooks of low branches for residues of pine resin. When he'd collected a few nuggets, he broke off three sturdy twigs the length of his forearm. He let the rucksack slide from his shoulders, opened it and began to tear off strips of fabric from the cotton liner of his sleeping bag.

Jasmine watched as he improvised a torch by wrapping pieces of sleeping bag liner, pine resin and handfuls of tissues from his jacket pockets around one of the thick twigs. After a minute she took something from her inside pocket. It was a spool of dental floss. 'Waxed,' she said quietly. 'Use it to tie everything on. It'll burn longer.'

When Ben was done, he stopped for a moment, allowed himself to look at Jasmine. Right into her eyes, as he hadn't dared in hours.

'I know it's scary,' Ben told her softly. 'We could go back, if you think it's too much. We'd have to go now though, because it'll take a while to get up that slope. Sometime tomorrow afternoon, GF One will start to wonder why we haven't been in touch. They'll send someone for us. We'd stand a good chance of making it until tomorrow at the hut, we can make a fire that would last a couple of hours. We could do that, if you like. Or, we could keep going. We've come a long way already. Inside the mountain, it'll be warmer; more insulated from the wind chill. Plus there's a very good chance that Rigel can find the way through these mountains. Look at him, he's raring to go. I promise you – he doesn't do that unless he's got a scent. Dogs don't like dark, enclosed spaces, either. But he's been trained to go crazy for a scent.'

She looked at him for a long time. Ben could see her weighing things up; her own anxieties, Rigel's odd behaviour, maybe even wondering how well she knew Ben.

'Sometimes you have to trust,' he said, his eyes on hers.

'All right,' she said. She began to nod. 'I trust you.'

Ben smiled. He handed her the lighter. 'Want to do the honours?' He held the torch he'd made out in front of Jasmine. She snapped a flame from the lighter and held it beneath one of the cotton strips of the torch. They watched the torch flare into life.

He turned to the dark crevice in the granite flank of the mountain. He clicked his tongue three times; the coded signal he'd trained Rigel to recognise.

Lead me.

— ICE TRAIL —

Ben hadn't been entirely honest.

He moved nervously through the narrow passageway, one hand on Jasmine's arm. Ahead, the flames of the torch cast dense shadows against smooth rock walls.

If there was one place in the mountains that Ben *really* hated to be, it was inside them.

Everything he knew about geology, Ben had learned from his mother on their frequent alpine hikes. The entire mountain range was glacial. Water had been inside these rocks once. It had swollen as it froze solid, cracking apart the granite to leave perfectly smooth walls with razor sharp edges. Over time, the edges had worn smooth. They were following an ancient ice trail.

With absolutely zero assurance that the passage wouldn't, at some point, dwindle to nothing.

Even though Jasmine had immediately seen the flaw in his plan, Ben hadn't admitted it. Just like he hadn't mentioned his mild claustrophobia, nor shared his fears with her about the troubling sounds they'd heard in the woods. He wasn't trying to be a smart-ass. At least, that's what Ben kept telling himself. He was just trying to keep the two of them thinking positively. Jasmine had seemed edgy from the beginning. Her nervousness kept threatening to infect him. He couldn't allow that.

Survival often boiled down to attitude – that's what Caroline had taught him. She'd rescued people in her youth, climbers who should have been dead. Exposed on the mountains overnight, they'd dug snow caves, hung on grimly and survived. Positivity – that was the key.

Maybe in the city, realism was a survival trait. But in the wilderness, realism too easily tipped into *fatalism*. And fatalism would kill you.

Rigel would only enter a cave if he'd picked up a scent – that much was true. But what Ben hadn't dared to admit to Jasmine was that Rigel hadn't been trained to signal the difference between a live scent trail and a dead one. It was one of the things that Ben had planned for this trip – to teach Rigel to signal via the wearable tech collar the moment he'd detected the tell-tale whiff of death.

Chemicals were given off after death that simply weren't present in a living person. A dog could be trained to recognise this.

Ben wasn't sure whether to regret that he wouldn't get the chance to train Rigel in this now – after all, a *living* scent trail was their best way of making it out of here.

The interior of the mountain never reached what Ben could think of as 'warm', but soon enough they were both unzipping their jackets. It was a relief not to have the chill biting into the exposed skin of his face.

The torch-fire began to die out. Ben handed the torch to Jasmine and took out a second stick, ripped more cotton from his sleeping-bag liner, added more pine resin and tied everything tightly with Jasmine's dental floss. He checked his watch. The first torch had lasted thirty-five minutes. They had two left.

In about seventeen minutes then, they'd be halfway through their light source.

He turned to Jasmine. 'If we don't find a way out in seventeen minutes, we turn back. OK?'

She looked confused for a moment, then angry. 'Turn back? I thought that wasn't an option any more.'

'Well, it soon won't be,' he said, ignoring the implied accusation. 'If we don't find some sign of a way out by then, we won't have enough torchlight to see our way back. It's dangerous out in the open, Jazz. But the truth is, we have more options outside. We can gather more firewood.'

He was starting to wonder if they shouldn't have just done that from the start; gathered firewood and waited it out in the hut.

'What if whoever took Paul decides to go back to the hut for us too?' Jasmine said, suddenly and with an intensity that surprised him. 'We've assumed that whoever took Paul and Rigel didn't care about us. But what if they just weren't expecting us to be there? I've been thinking about this, Ben. They must have got to Rigel first, or he'd have barked the second they came inside. They must have tempted him to go outside.

Drugged him, maybe with fresh meat? And then they came inside.'

Ben thought about this for a few seconds. 'If they were expecting Rigel, they had to have known about me. And anyway, they were probably following us.'

'Not necessarily,' she said. 'They could easily have known we were going to be at the hut – the agency who sets up the alpine huts could have told them. But maybe they were only expecting three people. Remember – I came along *only* at the last minute.'

It didn't seem likely to Ben. 'You think they left both of us because they didn't want to leave one of us alone?'

Jasmine shook her head firmly. 'I think maybe they didn't have space on the snowmobile for two more people. Just one. So they left. With plans to come back.'

'You're saying the hut might not be safe?' he said, slowly. He was a good deal more sceptical than he was letting her see.

'Don't sound so disappointed that you didn't think of it first,' she said teasingly, digging him in the stomach with the cold end of the dying torch. 'Hard-core military wannabe that you are, and all.'

'It's not that,' Ben said, lightly. 'It's just that I don't think they give a flying fig what happens to us. They took everything valuable, they took Paul. They left enough equipment to let us survive. *Ergo*, killing us wasn't their primary aim.'

'Who said anything about killing us?' she said. 'Surely we're more valuable alive – to kidnappers.'

'Kidnappers?' he said, unable to stop a hint of a sneer. 'Oh please.'

They began to walk forwards again. Rigel had returned, wagging his tail, looking up as if to say 'Where'd you get to?'

'It's one theory,' she said. 'What's yours, if you don't buy *kidnappers*?'

'I still think it's Paul Scott playing silly beggars.'

But Jasmine just gave a hollow laugh. 'Yeah, right. You're risking our lives for something you believe is a hoax.'

Ben couldn't look at her. She was right. And he should have thought about the possibility that whoever had taken Paul might come back for them. He'd been concentrating so fiercely on staying positive, Ben hadn't allowed himself to think through what might be going on. He'd assumed that Jasmine had been doing the same.

But no; it turned out that she'd been thinking strategically.

After a few more minutes, Ben stopped walking. 'All right,' he said. 'You've got a point. I admit it.'

'Why didn't you say so before?'

He didn't reply.

She hesitated. 'Was it because you didn't want me to worry?'

'Maybe.'

'Playing the hero?'

'Keeping focus,' he snapped. For a moment, he

almost felt angry. He was responsible for Jasmine. It was making him take different decisions to the ones he might take if he was alone with Rigel.

He checked his watch again. Twelve minutes before their torch light burned down to the halfway point. He began to stride even faster now, slowing only to slide through the narrower crevices in the wall.

The ceiling became suddenly and steeply lower. For most of the trail, they hadn't been able to see the upper reach of the cracks in the mountain. But now, the tunnel became tighter and smaller. And then they heard it.

Running water.

They stared at each other for an instant, then began to move as fast as they dared. In another two minutes they were standing on the banks of a wide underground river. Ben held the torch directly above the water, trying to gauge the depth.

'How deep?'

'Not sure. Probably too deep to wade,' he said.

Rigel appeared, back from some expedition along the river. He stood and barked a couple of times. But Ben couldn't tell what he meant. The barks sounded like vague encouragement to continue. Where to, he couldn't guess.

'The scent trail must run out here,' Ben said. 'Whoever Rigel was following must have gone into the water.'

Jasmine stuck one hand into the water, flinched and withdrew it. 'I don't think so. It's insanely cold.'

'They probably brought a canoe.'

'Oh yeah,' Jasmine said. 'Those little fibreglass tubs. I have one at home.'

'Looks like they stopped walking, got into their boat and headed downstream. Which means the stream probably comes out of the mountain at a safe height.'

She looked hard at him. 'You're not suggesting . . .'

He returned the gaze. 'Got any better ideas?'

Jasmine held her river-soaked hand to Ben's cheek. It felt like she'd been clutching ice. 'Feel that? That's after a couple of seconds. This water would kill us in a few minutes.'

'Then we'd better be close to where it comes out.'

She rocked back onto her heels, shaking her head.

Ben paused, licking his lips. There was an instant, sudden chill as a tiny cut in the skin of his lips was exposed to extra cold. The sensation gave him an idea. He stared at the flames of the torch. They were all blowing gently in one direction – upstream.

'Look,' he said. 'A breeze.' He pointed downstream. 'And it's coming from there. That's our way out – the water.'

⬤ FREEZE ⬤

Ben peered into the gloom. The river cut through the rock, which rose at least three metres high in places. The question was – for how long?

He edged sideways along the narrow ledge that bordered the river on their side, until the ledge disappeared and he hit a wall of rock that went flush to the water. Was there a similar ledge on the opposite bank? The torch didn't cast more than ten metres of light. After that it was just blackness. The ceiling might drop, or even disappear.

A freezing underground swim, with no light or knowledge of how far they'd have to go? Sounded pretty much like a below-zero version of hell.

There wasn't much time to think about it. Every second they stood still, the torch was burning their time. Ben removed his rucksack, then his jacket. He pulled off the microfleece beneath. Out of the corner of his eye, he could see Jasmine staring at him. He tried not to look back.

'That tin of lip balm,' he said. 'Can you get it out?'

Jasmine was sliding her rucksack from her shoulders now, following his lead and removing her outer clothes.

'We're going to have to get fairly, you know . . .'

Ben admitted, awkwardly, still not looking at her. 'Put our clothes in the rucksack, tie the rucksacks in the bin liners. Smear some lip balm on your chest and back, around your core. It'll take the edge off the cold.'

She was incredulous. 'We're seriously going to do this?'

A shudder ran through him as he remembered her icy hand on his cheek. This was going to be really, really horrible.

He was down to his boxers, stuffing all his clothes into the rucksack. Now he was shivering for real. She handed him her tin of lip balm. Their eyes met for a moment and he held his gaze there, determined not to allow Jasmine to see him taking in as much as he dared of her in this unclothed state. It wasn't like seeing a girl in swimwear. She looked slim, slight and *utterly* vulnerable. He took about half of what was in the tin and rubbed it between both hands, warming the grease. Then he covered his chest with it, reaching around to get as much on his back as he could. Jasmine, he noted, did the same. She hadn't uttered a word of complaint.

She trusted him. The thought was like a hard kick, made him ache from the dread it triggered within.

This was how it would be if he joined Gemini Force. People would have to trust him with their lives, all the time. Sometimes, he wouldn't be able to save them. Some of them would die.

Maybe even today.

Last chance to change your mind.

But the pinch of pain in his lip was a constant reminder, and now the chill of his exposed skin. There was definitely a breeze. The outside could not be far away. When their rucksacks were safely inside tightly knotted bin liners, Ben nodded.

'Don't jump in; ease in gently. It's grim, I know, but you have to minimise the shock.'

To his surprise, she slid in almost gracefully, and then reached for her bag. Before he could move, Jasmine was already gliding down the river. Apart from the occasional gasp, she didn't make a sound.

He turned to Rigel. This was going to be the real test. A human being could be coaxed into freezing water. A dog couldn't.

Ben had a special command for Rigel, one that would force the dog to enter scary places; situations that would challenge his very instincts. Once a week he'd used it to get Rigel to leap off the helicopter platform and into the open ocean above GF One.

There was little more terrifying to a dog than open water. For Rigel, it was especially scary. He still had memories of their ordeal in the capsized, burning oil platform, Horizon Alpha. But after a solid six days, Rigel had finally submitted to Ben's command.

'Rigel, *leap of faith*.'

The dog whined with that mixture of sorrow and obedience that always plucked at Ben's heart. The dog walked straight into the water and began to paddle.

There was no more time. Ben eased himself into the

water. Every centimetre of his skin felt like it was encased in fire. The cold burn was relentless, inescapable. Now he understood why Jasmine hadn't spoken. Speech felt impossible. His nervous system seemed to close down every function except forward motion and occasionally, breathing. His air came in gulps, erratic. He held the torch aloft, dragging his own bin liner parcel with his left hand.

Every second that passed was pure, screaming pain. Every so often he'd hear the agony in one of Jasmine's gasps or his own. It might have been comical, if it didn't hurt so much.

'One day,' he eventually managed to mutter between chattering teeth, 'we'll . . . laugh . . . about this.'

The fact that she even managed a chuckle was like an instant burst of warmth.

Between them, Rigel paddled steadily. He was such a good swimmer now, Ben realised, with pride.

'A ledge,' Jasmine sputtered.

'Oh thank *Christ*,' Ben replied, shakily. 'Hurry. Can . . . hardly feel . . . my legs.'

He could see the ledge now. Jasmine had just reached it, was dragging herself out. Rigel was next, leaping out of the water and, as he'd been trained to do, removing himself to a safe distance before he shook himself violently.

At least Ben didn't need to worry about Rigel freezing. But for him and Jasmine, every second now counted. They had to dress and warm up as fast as possible.

Ben laid a hand on the ledge, which was almost two metres deep at this point, with a tunnel leading away. He hoped desperately that Rigel didn't want them to enter that tunnel. The desire to see natural light again was surging within him now, almost overpowering.

Panic would be next.

Then he pulled himself out onto the ledge, somehow managing to keep his chest from touching the cold, wet surface of the rock. Rigel had ambled back now, and without a second thought Ben said to Jasmine, 'Lie down on your back. I'm going to get Rigel to warm you up. Just relax, don't be scared.'

Then to Rigel he said, curtly, 'Rigel, *St Bernard*!'

The dog padded over to Jasmine and sat down over her chest. After a moment's hesitation, Ben watched as she embraced him with both arms.

'Doggy, you smell gross,' she said, her voice trembling, face buried in Rigel's fur.

Ben's hands shook uncontrollably as he untied the knot in his bin liner. Eventually he managed to get into his rucksack and pull his microfleece over his chest. The relief was incredible. He was dressed in another minute, sitting down to pull his socks on, when Jasmine began to push Rigel away.

'I'm OK now,' she said. Ben grabbed her bin liner and swiftly untied it. He passed her the fleece first, then the rest of her clothes.

Their teeth were still clattering together as they stood up a few minutes later, fully dressed. Ben looked at her for a moment, wishing that he could risk a long hug. But she had a boyfriend. He wasn't sure what the rules were about these things. Jasmine had hugged him when his mother died – was that how bad things had to get before it was allowed?

Ugh. Stupid rules.

Forgotten on the ground, the torch faded to a glow, and went out. Ben was about to curse, when he realised that he could still see Jasmine – just. Her eyes shimmered occasionally, and there was a ghostly light around her face.

'Light!' they both said, at the same time. It was coming from downstream. The river narrowed sharply as they began to follow the ledge. The ceiling became lower too. At the end of the darkness, about ten metres away, the remains of the day's sunlight illuminated the water. It looked like a silver-blue stained glass window – not more than a metre high and maybe two metres wide, a third of which was the narrow rock ledge.

They'd have to crawl, but they could get out. Without torchlight. And most importantly, soon.

Ben went first, preparing himself for the potential disappointment of being trapped high up on a rock face. When he finally poked his head into the open, he couldn't hold back his delight.

They were in a valley, picturesque as any he'd ever seen in the Alps, a mountain stream, bursting from a crack in the rock, and meandering towards a small glacial lake. Such a pretty spot would be sure to attract the usual Swiss attention of a barbecue station complete with freshly chopped pine and a picnic area, trails and a car park.

Ten minutes later Ben was negotiating a ride with a couple of tourists who agreed to run him, Jasmine and Rigel down to the nearest village in exchange for some petrol money.

'Just one thing though,' Ben added, as they climbed into the back of a Volvo. 'Can I borrow a phone?'

He could feel Jasmine's eyes on him as he dialled. Mouth dry, he raised the phone to his ear, waiting for someone at GF One to pick up.

'Hi,' he began, breathlessly. 'It's me – Ben.'

There was a slight pause. 'G'day, Ben,' came Paul's voice. 'Nice going. I had fifty francs said you'd call before dinner. You just won me enough to get some serious Toblerone. So, mate, where the heck are you?'

⏜ SIXTEEN ⏜

'Your voice,' Addison said, tears rolling down her cheeks. 'Your face!' She wiped her face with her wrist. 'I know I shouldn't. Seriously. It's a good thing we were over a hundred metres away or I'm pretty sure you'd have heard us laugh.'

'Take no notice of Addi,' Paul advised, his eyes on the road ahead. 'Fighting in Afghanistan seems to have twisted her mind. *I* wasn't laughing. It wasn't an easy thing, what we put you through.'

Ben smiled. From the second he'd heard Paul's voice answer the GF One emergency line, all the anxieties and stress had washed away. He'd been right after all – it had been a test.

'I knew it,' he said, turning to Jasmine. 'Didn't I say?'

Jasmine gave a vague nod before turning to press her forehead against the glass of the window. She seemed preoccupied. Not as happy as Ben was to find out that it had been a test, which he'd passed with flying colours.

'Truby wanted a realistic assessment of how well you've trained Rigel to perform in the field. If we're going to trust him to lead you into rescue situations, we need to know he's reliable.'

For a second, Ben was astonished. 'Wait – so this wasn't about testing *me*?'

Paul shook his head. 'You? Ben, you've already proved yourself a couple of times over. I'd be dead if it weren't for you. *And* those blokes from Horizon Alpha.'

'Your dog, on the other hand, he's an unknown quantity.' Addison reached into the passenger seat, ruffling Rigel's left ear. 'But Benedict trained you up pretty good, didn't he, poochy?'

Ben put a protective arm around the dog. 'Please don't call him "poochy".'

'Good point,' Paul said. 'I guess he's gonna be part of the team now. Maybe he should get a zodiac name.'

'What? I don't even have one of those!' objected Ben. 'Anyhow, he's already named after a star – in the constellation of Orion.'

Their laughter made him realise that yet again, the Gemini Force team members were lightly teasing him.

'Well, I don't care if the test was for Rigel. Far as I'm concerned, Jazz is the real hero here. She helped me to stay calm, didn't show any fear.'

Jasmine released a quiet gasp, as if she was wincing from pain. She couldn't seem to meet Ben's gaze. For a moment he was puzzled. And then he understood.

'Oh,' he said, deflated. 'You knew. Didn't you? Of course you did. What was I thinking? Dietz wouldn't have sent you on a trip like that if you didn't know.'

Voice muffled against the glass of the window, Jasmine replied. 'They needed me to play along. Ben

. . .' She turned slightly, just enough to be able to look at him, sideways on. To Ben's astonishment, he noticed that her eyes were glistening with fresh, unshed tears. He reached, instinctively, to brush her cheek with the back of his hand. Jasmine's tears fell then, trickled along his index finger.

'I'm sorry,' she managed to whisper, barely able to look at him.

Caught awkwardly in the gesture, Ben held his fingers to her cheek, daring to move them in the gentlest of caresses. 'Hey!' he murmured. 'It's OK. You were only trying to help.'

'I hated lying to you,' she muttered.

For a moment, he looked at her, closely. The truth was, he'd been upset to realise that Jasmine had lied to him. But her reaction, her disappointment in herself, was utterly disarming. He knew her well enough to know that nothing about *this* was fabricated. If Paul and Addison hadn't been in the car with them, Ben would have hugged her.

'It's a very good thing you guys chose to follow the river out of there. If you'd taken the other tunnel, you could have been in there for days. You certainly do know your mountains, Carrington,' Addison said, apparently oblivious to what was going on between Ben and Jasmine. 'I'll give you that.'

Ben, Addison and Paul spent New Year's Eve as guests of Jasmine and Michael Dietz, watching the spectacular laser and firework show in the centre of Bern before flying back to GF One on the first day of the new year. As exciting as it was to see the base emerge from the cylinder of 'invisibility' that encased it during daytime appearances above the sea, Ben preferred the drama of a night-time arrival.

How must it look to a distant observer who might catch a transient glimpse, perhaps from the window of a passenger jet? There'd be a sudden explosion of a circle of blue lights, as straight as lasers, flashing for just a second or two. Then they'd seem to blink out of existence for a second, dimming to a pale reminder of what had been there before. Just enough to guide in a helicopter, or one of Gemini Force's specialised rescue vehicles, all of them coming in to land on areas that gave little room for error.

But that small amount of room was enough, because Gemini Force's aerial pilots had proved themselves to be some of the best, most agile, fearless in the world; hand-picked from the air forces of the USA, Australia, Japan and Brazil.

The Sikorsky S-76 descended into the base's heli-pad to a riot of balloons – pink, silver and white. A huge banner was draped across the ceiling of the mezzanine level. It read HAPPY BIRTHDAY, JASMINE.

The conference room was open, the table laid with a simple, white damask tablecloth and covered with plates of food. There were pieces of grilled steak, fish tacos and other local Mexican delicacies, potato and rice salads and two enormous cakes – one chocolate and the other, a vanilla cheesecake.

At the threshold, Ben turned to Jasmine, once again astonished at how she'd kept information from him. 'You're sixteen . . . today, on New Year's Day?'

She smiled, bashful. 'Next week. But my time with Dad ends on the third. I'm having another party back at Mom's, in Geneva.'

'Ah – the proper party,' Ben said. 'The one with all your friends.'

'Not all. *You're* my friend,' she said, looking directly into his eyes. 'Although I guess that's hard to believe, now that you know I lied to you.'

Ben's fingers twitched, eager to reach for Jasmine's hand and squeeze until he'd convinced her that it was forgotten. But Tim and Paul pushed past them both, boisterously exclaiming at the sight before them.

She managed a nervous grin, picked up two plates and passed one to him. 'We should start before they eat everything.'

Ben piled his plate high and began to circulate. He'd been away from the base for five days in total, including a flying visit to the empty Brandis family home he'd inherited, in Austria. Before that though, he'd lived pretty much solidly on GF One, ever since the end of October.

Even though space on GF One was limited, it never became claustrophobic. Odd, considering how sensitive he was to that feeling. Maybe it was the vastness of the sea that surrounded them?

At night, he felt cosy and safe inside the base. Outside was pitch black – the depths of the sea. During the day, a delicious blue light permeated the entire base from the moment the sun rose high enough in the sky. Ben found he'd grown to love the varying shades of blue as the hours passed. It was calming, peaceful.

The changing environments of the base, whose decor Addison had laughed at the first time they'd both seen it, turned out to be particularly cheering. Sometimes Ben enjoyed nothing more than taking a mug of hot chocolate and plonking himself on one of the chintzy sofas in the living area. It felt a little like being in one of the slightly dilapidated rooms of the Brandis country house; brought back happy memories of his mother, Caroline.

Even happy memories could be painful, Ben was realising. But at least when he felt that pain, he felt her presence.

Just then, GF One's chief of medicine, Nina Atalas, approached. With her was someone Ben hadn't seen before – a guy. He had pale olive-brown skin, very dark eyes, about five feet nine, black hair styled with gel, perfectly rumpled. On his nose was a pair of stylish black and metal-framed glasses that gave him a cool air of geek-chic. He looked young – maybe even a teenager, and was obviously dressed for the party – a crisp, tailored, black-and-purple striped shirt over designer jeans, a pair of pristine orange-and-black trainers on his feet, a brand so undoubtedly hipster that Ben didn't even recognise it.

'Ben, this is my son, Denny,' Nina said. The guy balled up his hand, ready to bump fists with Ben. Awkwardly, Ben did the same.

'Hey, my man,' Denny said, smoothly. 'So you're the new recruit. Sweet.'

'Denny's a freshman at Columbia,' Nina told Ben. 'In New York.'

Ben had heard of the university. Some of the boys at school were applying to Ivy League colleges in the USA. He guessed that Denny was probably eighteen, at least. But in the next breath, Denny made sure to tell him that no, he was some kind of genius, had been accepted into the university when he was fifteen and had actually taken a year off before starting.

'This is your "gap year"?' Denny asked. There was a patronising edge to his tone. Nina excused herself with a gracious smile, leaving the two boys alone.

Denny's voice instantly lowered. 'OK, now you can dish the goods on Jasmine. Is she with anyone? 'Cause she is *smokin'*.' He adjusted his glasses, self-consciously. 'Am I right, or am I right?'

Ben resisted the urge to glance across the mezzanine level at Jasmine, who stood with her father and Truby, cutting cake.

'She's got a boyfriend,' he said, curtly.

Denny gave a single shake of his head. 'Not that Jonah kid?'

Ben nodded. 'Yup. Believe so.'

'That jerk; he's been trailing after her for like, a

year. That's really not fair. Dude should move over, let someone else cut in.'

'Don't be idiotic. It's not a dance.'

Denny stared at Ben, a red plastic cup in one hand, a wicked grin all over his face. 'Not a dance? Oh, boy. Clueless!'

'Tell me, Denny, what do you do at Columbia?' Ben said, leaning forward confidently. He wasn't going to be talked to like that by this guy, child prodigy or not.

'Math and computer science.'

Ben turned away so Denny wouldn't catch his eye-roll.

Of course you do.

━ TRUBY ━

Everyone that Ben wanted to talk to was over on the other side of the deck. Now Jasmine, Dietz and Truby were joined by the junior medic, twenty-five-year-old Cuban-American, Lola Reyes. Meanwhile, Denny seemed content to have trapped Ben, pouring punch into his party cup and banging on about how popular he was with the girls at Columbia University.

Ben's eyes kept going to the table with the cake, around which Jasmine and Lola still hovered.

'You're into Doctor Lola,' Denny said, suddenly. When Ben glanced at him, sharply, there was a ready smile to greet his surprise. 'Least, that's what I heard. True? Or am I being suckered?'

'Where'd you hear that?'

Denny shrugged. 'The pilots, they say stuff.'

'Oh,' Ben said, his skin prickling slightly in embarrassment and annoyance. 'They should know better.'

'Really? I heard you had a crush, used to text Lola all the time, back when you were at boarding school.'

It was true, and Ben had no answer for this. If someone else had asked him, Addison or Toru maybe, he'd have been honest, admitted that it had been a fleeting crush.

But to Denny? No way. 'Someone's got a big mouth,' he said, acidly.

'Ah,' Denny said, with a satisfied smile. 'It *is* true. Hey, no judgement, buddy. There are older girls at school I like; girls in their final year. I totally get it. Me, I prefer them my age, or a little younger. I like a girl who'll look up to me; you know, a girl I can impress.'

Ben shot Denny a look of pure disdain. 'Talk a lot of guff, don't you?'

Denny didn't miss a beat. 'Not sure I know what "guff" is, "old boy",' he said, imitating Ben's English accent. 'But I get the sense you're not real comfortable on the topic, so let's move on.'

Ben placed his cup on the nearest countertop. 'Sounds good to me. I'll see you later.'

He stalked off, headed at first towards Jasmine and Lola, but when he heard the snigger from Denny behind him, Ben swerved and changed direction, aiming for Tim and Toru.

He didn't get that far. Truby's voice called him back to the central table, where Jasmine was completely engrossed in conversation with Lola, who also didn't give Ben a second glance.

When he heard Jasmine mention the name 'Jonah', Ben's head turned, for a second. Then he forced himself to ignore it. Only morons like Denny allowed themselves to become obsessed with girls.

'We should catch up,' Truby said, lightly tapping Ben

on the shoulder. 'You and Rigel made a great team, I hear.'

Ben nodded, a little warily. He still had half an eye and ear on Jasmine's conversation with Lola. Jonah, according to Jasmine, was being 'kind of a pain'.

Truby asked, 'Where is Rigel?'

Ben hooked a thumb towards the soft furnishings of the living room area. Rigel was curled up with a marrowbone, devotedly licking the edge and interior.

'Good one.' Truby chuckled. 'He deserves a reward. How about you, Ben; think you deserve one?'

'I'm just trying to make myself useful,' Ben replied with a shrug. But he couldn't help thinking that yes, he'd begun to contribute to Gemini Force, at least enough to merit a uniform.

Truby laughed, this time clapping a firmer hand to the boy's shoulder. 'I'm quite certain that you do deserve some kind of reward. So, tomorrow morning, Ben, what do you say to taking your first helicopter flying lesson – with yours truly?'

The instant that Ben, stammering, agreed to this amazing and unexpected offer, Truby darted off to talk to Julia and Paul. Spotting Ben once more alone, Denny sauntered over. Ben sighed. What was up with this guy? He was kind of creepy.

'Did I hear that right – Truby's going to take you for a lesson in the Sikorsky?'

Ben drew himself to his full height – a few centimetres

taller than Denny, he noted with satisfaction. 'I've been on at him to let me have a go.'

'Good for you,' Denny nodded, approvingly. 'Enjoy it. There's nothing quite like your first time.'

Ben found himself staring incredulously at Denny. 'You're learning to fly too?'

'Started six months ago,' the teenager confirmed. He continued, in a lofty tone. 'I went out with Truby, a while back. He's a good teacher. We had a great conversation about business. I'm planning on doing an MBA in a couple years, so I figured, y'know, get a head start with making contacts, am I right? We talked about how he got started, how he built up Trubycom, his partnership with that scientific genius, Professor Gerald Anderson, all that. Quite a story,' Denny said, stuffing a forkful of cheesecake into his mouth. Slightly muffled, he continued, 'But he's probably told you?'

Ben didn't even bother to mask his annoyance this time. 'No,' he said, coldly. 'We never talk about business. I'm not bothered about how Jason made his money. Only with what he chooses to do with it – right here on GF One.'

They met at the helipad the next morning at eight. Truby arrived a couple of minutes after him, sipping from a tall insulated cup. 'Gotta have my coffee,' he said with a slightly embarrassed smile. 'OK, son, let's do this.' He tapped on a small control panel in the wall, then stood back as the wall rolled back, exposing the parked Sikorsky S-76. Ben could just see the second chopper in the reserve space, around the back of the helipad.

For a second, they just stood there. Then Truby gestured at the helicopter with his free hand. 'Lead the way.'

Somewhat nervously, Ben approached the Sikorsky, opened the door and let himself into the main pilot's seat. The chopper could be flown from either of two front positions, but Ben assumed that he'd be learning to fly as a pilot today, not as a co-pilot.

To Ben's relief, Truby didn't correct him, just smiled, sat in the co-pilot seat and buckled up.

Ben positioned his feet carefully on the two rudder pedals. He began to look at the controls, touching everything once, gently, getting accustomed to the positions, to the hand movements between the cyclic, the collective and the navaids on the instrument panel.

He'd never actually sat in this position before – not for real. But he'd put time in on the simulator program for the S-76. Truby had been hinting for a couple of weeks now that since Ben was sixteen, he was eligible to be trained to fly a helicopter.

Hints were all very well, but Ben wanted things to happen as fast as possible. He had less than a year to prove himself. If things went really well, if Ben could become indispensable, there was a chance that Truby would not make him return to school the following September.

It had only been a couple of months but already the thought of going back to school made Ben feel physically ill. The possibility of any future that wasn't Gemini Force filled his heart with an exquisite ache. Ben didn't understand why. 'Sometimes you seem a little over-anxious,' Nina had once told him. 'Maybe we should take some time, talk about it?'

But Ben wasn't interested in talking about it, or analysing his feelings. He just knew that every morning he woke up with a number in his mind: the exact number of days left for him to demonstrate his worth to Jason Truby.

There were days when the sheer improbability of it all really hit Ben. What were the odds that Truby would allow a guy who hadn't even finished high school a shot – a real shot – at joining Gemini Force?

Those days, Ben felt the weight of every minute. But mostly, he was optimistic. He'd promised Truby that he'd work hard, 24/7, to make himself worthy of the team.

Not a day went by when Ben didn't remind himself of that promise.

━ COZUMEL ━

He'd never felt a rush quite like it.

This time, it was Ben who roused the sleeping leviathan that was GF One. It was Ben who brought it to the surface of the Caribbean Sea, staring through the helicopter window at waterfalls of teal-coloured water spilling around him.

Unforgettable.

Truby reminded him, lightly, to take control of the Sikorsky. Ben gripped the collective firmly in his left hand. He began to raise it.

The helicopter lifted gently off the heli-pad. It hovered a metre above the surface.

Ben adjusted the throttle by twisting the end of the collective, increasing the engine speed. One foot leaned on the left pedal. The chopper rose higher in the air. With his right hand on the cyclic, he pushed forward. As the Sikorsky transitioned from vertical to forward motion, it shuddered slightly. The helicopter began to fly forwards. In another two seconds, it had cleared GF One altogether.

Confidence coursed through him. He'd executed the take-off almost exactly as he'd practised. Casually, Ben spoke into his radio headset. 'Beecee to One, we're clear of the base.'

He couldn't exactly remember when they'd started using his initials as his radio call sign. Until he finally earned a zodiac call sign, he accepted that 'Beecee' would have to do.

Behind them, Ben could hear the roar of suction above the sound of the rotor blades as GF One returned to the depths. Water rushed in everywhere, creating a satisfyingly throaty rumble.

You never heard that sound when you were inside the base.

Inside, you could forget just *how* magnificent a piece of aquatic engineering GF One truly was. The interior was designed to feel like a cross between an underwater firefighting station and the offices of a hipster-filled Silicon Valley software company. But the exterior was smooth, curved, with a matt finish to the metallic paint that mimicked the blues of the ocean and the flesh tones of a coral reef. There were dozens of moving parts, ballast that filled and emptied to move the base up and down along anchors in the shallow trench below the base.

It wasn't strictly Ben's first time flying a helicopter. That had been an altogether more terrifying event. He could still remember the cold sweats when he'd been told by Addison to take the controls of GF Three – usually known as *Scorpio* – Gemini Force's only helicopter-like custom-built craft. He'd flown *Scorpio*, strictly under the pilot's instructions, whilst next to him, Addi herself had flown the stranded *Aquarius*, by remote.

That had been something of an ordeal. By comparison, today was a stroll on the beach. Pure pleasure. Ben could feel the vibrations of the rotor blade through the cyclic, the growl of the throttle.

'Don't be the pilot,' Addison had told him. 'Be the *aircraft*. It'll come alive for you, if you'll let it breathe. Every physical force exerts some pressure, somewhere. *You* are the biological component in the machine. You can sense everything.'

When he pitched the craft forward just slightly, Ben felt the change of angle, the new bite to the air as it whispered past. Totally fixated on the metallic blue of the waves below them, Ben scarcely heard Truby's admiring murmur; 'Good, Ben. You're doing well.'

The east coast of Cozumel came into sight.

'Where are we headed?' Ben asked. 'Truby Central?'

It was the crew's nickname for the luxury villa that Truby owned on the unfashionable side of the Mexican island. Hurricanes and exposure to the open waters of the Caribbean meant that very few islanders chose to live there. Truby's closest neighbour, a retired mining engineer named Mario Torres, was two kilometres away.

Truby Central was the only place on Cozumel that Ben had ever been, aside from the airport.

Truby shook his head, a mild, almost secretive grin on his lips. 'No . . . don't think so. I think I'd like you to head across the island, circle around a little. Let's see how you do at landing in a narrow clearing.'

At Truby's words Ben felt a sweat break out all over the back of his neck. He'd assumed that Truby would land the craft. Truby must have noticed the catch in Ben's breath, because he put his sunglasses on and beamed.

'Look at that surf. It's high – four, five metres. Check out the length of that swell. I bet we got some barrelling going on. Oh yeah, I thought so, look, there are at least five guys out there. Did you ever surf, Ben? I tried a few times when I was a young man. But it's really kind of a lifestyle choice.'

Now it seemed that Truby wasn't even talking to Ben, but to himself. 'Wave chaser. Yeah. That could have been something.' He glanced at Ben, eyes away from the vision of whitecaps in the sea beneath them. Softly he said, 'The road not travelled, eh, Ben?'

Ben risked only a quick look down at the waves, then pulled his eyes back to the controls. There was so much to remember. Truby was acting as though they did this every day. But Ben's nerve endings tingled on high alert.

'You wish you'd been a surfer?' Ben managed to say.

It intrigued Ben that Jason Truby ever contemplated anything other than the path he'd taken – electronic engineer, software designer, entrepreneur – to billionaire and one-time astronaut. Would Ben himself ever look back at his own life in the same way and wonder?

Somewhere in the back of his throat, Truby chuckled. He smoothed one hand over his neat scrub of silver-and-black hair, and made a 'hmmm' sound. As though he were weighing up the question in his mind. But Ben never did get an answer, because at that moment, the on-board radio crackled.

'Jason Truby, this is Mario Torres. Did I just see your Sikorsky fly over?'

Truby grabbed the radio handset. 'Mario, hey neighbour. What's up?'

Ben could hear the instant drop in the man's voice. 'Jason, man, I could use your help.'

To Ben's astonishment, there was an unmistakeable sob on the other end of the line.

'It's Richie,' continued Mario Torres. 'He's missing. He went on a hike with some classmates. At some point, they got into an argument and he went off by himself. The other two boys turned up last night. But it's been nine hours since they got home. And Richie is still somewhere out there.'

Truby said, 'Have you called the cops?'

'Yes, of course, but they won't act until he's been missing for twenty-four hours. Given the way the boys separated, and how close they were to the edge of the jungle, the cops don't think we need to worry yet.'

'But you're worried?'

On the other end of the radio there was an audible tremor in the man's voice. 'Jason, I'm scared. Richie is a good boy, a great hiker. Probably the best of the three boys who went out. I'm really worried that something bad has happened to him.'

'We can take a look for him,' Truby said.

'Jason, that's what I was praying you would say. I saw your chopper fly past and I thought, hey, maybe Jason can fly around over the place where Richie went missing.'

'Is Richie smart enough to know we'd be looking? I mean, would he know to make some kind of signal?'

Truby's neighbour seemed eager to reassure him. 'Sure, most definitely he would.'

'OK, Mario, email me your boy's last known coordinates, anything at all you can tell me about the route he was taking. Make it quick though – send the coordinates through first.'

As soon as Truby ended the conversation, he sat back and grasped his own cyclic with his right hand. 'Ben, hope you don't mind if I take over? We're going to need some precision flying. I need you to take over the comms station.'

With that, Ben sensed the flight controls on his side going dead as they were over-ridden. Truby nodded in the direction of his tablet computer, lodged in a holder on the instrument panel.

'My email account is open. When Mario's message comes through, I want you to program those coordinates into the navaids.'

Ben nodded curtly, fingers at the ready.

Eight-thirty in the morning and Ben had already enjoyed a bit of solo fly-time. Now he was out on a rescue mission. He allowed himself a tiny grin.

Not a bad start to the day.

⚊ JUNGLE ⚊

'If he's in there we'll never find him.'

Minutes had passed since Ben last saw a single break in the dense vegetation on the ground. Once you went into the interior, it was a tangle of low trees. If there was a hiking trail anywhere close by, you couldn't spot it from the ground.

They'd started the search by flying over the meagre ruins of a Mayan city at San Gervasio, in the middle of the island. The hikers had arrived by car, visited the ruins and then hiked a trail that led to the east coast. It was an ambitious route, popular with survivalist types who enjoyed the challenge of living off the land, or at least pretending to try. Once you reached the pure white beaches of the deserted eastern coast, you were meant to walk around to the more populous side of the island, surviving only on whatever could be salvaged from the sea and surrounding forest.

Two hours from the coast, the kids had argued about which route to take. Richie had taken a different path. That was the last his friends had seen of him.

The friends had tried to estimate on a map the position at which their paths had diverged. Truby had flown the Sikorsky three times over the same region.

Ben had found the trail and they'd followed it as far as it went. Then it appeared to peter out.

They searched in vain for another trail.

'I have a bad feeling about this,' muttered Truby. He swung the helicopter around, flying back the way they'd come.

'What should we do?'

Ben felt the helicopter judder into vertical motion. They began to descend above a narrow clearing. Ben recognised it as the crossroads where the kids had separated. It looked barely wide enough to allow the craft to land.

'We're gonna take a look,' Truby replied, briskly.

The landing was neatly executed, although Ben spotted the remains of a few shredded leaves floating to the ground in their wake. The rotors were still whirring when Truby stepped out. Ben unbuckled hurriedly and followed, hands over his lowered head.

Truby was opening the passenger section. He emerged a couple of seconds later with two small rucksacks. He tossed one over to Ben before putting his own over his shoulders.

'Basic survival equipment. You don't step out into any wilderness without it.'

They set off down the trail that they'd seen wither to nothing about five hundred metres along. Once they'd reached the dead end, they split up to examine the surrounding thicket. Ben had never been inside the rainforest or jungle before. He was surprised at how loud it was. They were five kilometres from the nearest road, but the racket of jungle insects was impressive.

'Richie must have gone back,' Truby concluded, after they'd searched the area for almost thirty minutes. 'Retraced his steps. There's no sign that anyone was here.'

'But we flew over the entire trail on the way over here,' objected Ben.

'Then I guess we missed something.'

'There's no way to get lost,' Ben said. 'Either you're on a trail or you're not. It's impossible to move more than ten metres in this forest.'

'It's not impossible, just really difficult. But I agree,' Truby said. 'Why would anyone want to – if they could use the trail?'

They returned to the helicopter. Truby was busying himself with replacing the rucksacks. Ben took a few moments to study the second path, the one the other boys had taken. He started walking down the trail and stopped when he heard Truby calling. Just as he turned, Ben noticed a shaft of light somewhere to his left, in the thicket. It was another clearing – a tiny one – but displaced from the trail by at least ten metres.

'Hang on,' Ben called back to Truby. 'I'm just going to check something out.'

He came off the path, picked his way painstakingly through gnarled branches, slapping at the occasional mosquito that landed on his face. He was thankful for the sturdy denim of his jeans – the undergrowth was positively tearing at his clothes.

Ben reached the second clearing. It was no more than two metres wide – a tiny oasis of light in the dense forest. And he saw it immediately – another, very narrow trail.

He rushed back the way he'd come or close enough. By the time Ben reached the helicopter his heart was pumping, his Rock Snakes T-shirt was soaked with sweat, the backs of his hands were covered in bites and scratches. Truby was in the pilot seat, doors of the craft open, waiting.

'There's another trail,' Ben said, panting slightly from the exertion. 'It's so narrow, we almost missed it. Hardly a trail, really. More a few machete swipes. I had a look at some of the cuts on the trees. They felt fresh.'

'We're gonna go back to base,' Truby said, in a determined voice. 'Get Rigel, a couple of the guys. Climb aboard, Ben.'

A crackle somewhere deep in the forest was followed instantly by the metallic sound of a bullet thudding into the aluminium shell of the helicopter. Ben froze for a millisecond. The moment he regained control of his muscles, he launched himself towards the open door of the Sikorsky.

A second bullet smacked into the bulletproof glass of the windscreen. It missed Ben's head by no more than a hand's width.

From inside the thicket came a faint voice.

'Tell your boy not to move, Mister Truby. I'm a good

shot but if he's gonna go scooting all over the place . . .'

Ben could feel his pulse racing even harder. They'd used Truby's name.

They *knew* him.

Ben's and Truby's presence in the forest today – it wasn't a coincidence.

Inside the helicopter, he could see Truby's expression of fury and resignation. He could hear him swearing loudly, mostly at himself.

Two minutes later, the sniper emerged from the forest. He looked to be a Mexican guy in his late twenties, a neat haircut and stylish stubble. He wore khaki fatigues and a jungle camouflage vest that exposed the hard muscles of his arms. The rifle was slung over his shoulder now, but he had a chunky looking automatic handgun in his right hand. From his waist hung an unsheathed machete.

The man looked every inch the professional killer.

As he approached, he actually smiled. Not a cruel smile but one of apparently genuine friendship. When he did, he revealed two rows of smooth, even teeth – every one of them golden. The weirdness of it gave Ben a jolt – a solid gold smile and a gun pointed right at his heart.

'Mister Truby, would you be so kind as to join your boy here?' called the sniper. He nodded at Ben. 'Who're you, kid? The latest 'nephew'? Is your mom Truby's new girl?'

With noticeable reluctance, Truby joined Ben outside

the helicopter. He shot Ben a single, almost apologetic look.

'Jason Truby, what an honour!' said the sniper. His lips pulled back tightly over the solid gold grille.

'Yeah, yeah, get it over with,' Truby said. 'How much do you want?'

'That's the question isn't it?' the sniper said, his English flawless, if slightly accented. 'Too much and I know you'll send for the cavalry. Too little and I miss out.'

'Where's Richie?' Truby said, ignoring the man's attempt at humour.

'He's a little tied up right now,' smirked the sniper.

'Does your boss know you're out here?' Truby said, a flame of anger in his eyes.

'My boss? Let me worry about my boss. He's always supported an entrepreneurial attitude.'

'Entrepreneur?' ventured Ben, scornfully. 'Is that what kidnappers are calling themselves these days?'

The sniper jerked a finger at Ben, looked towards Truby and chuckled. 'Hey – a funny one!'

Then without warning, he slammed his left fist into Ben's ribs. The blow was thunderingly hard. Ben felt a flare of pain in his side. He doubled up for a moment, fighting hard to recover his composure.

'It's all business,' the sniper said, lightly. 'If you want to live amongst us, rich man, you got to be prepared to pay the tax.'

Truby glanced at Ben for less than a second, his

expression unreadable. 'When I moved to Cozumel, people like you were still working out of Colombia.'

'Maybe we arrived a little late,' said the man, shrugging. 'But we got here, eventually. And now, *señor*, it's tax-collecting time.'

'How much?'

'That'll be twenty million US dollars. Oh – and the helicopter. Although I'm more than happy to give you a ride back to your place.'

The sniper beamed wider than ever, his gold-plated smile dazzling in the sunlight. 'Do we have a deal?'

'Twenty million?' Ben sputtered.

The friendly grin fell from the sniper's face. In its place was a puzzled frown. 'Don't you know who this Truby guy is? Wow – I guess your mom must be a pretty dedicated gold-digger. She didn't even clue you in on the score. That's small change, to him.'

Then his eyes went back to Truby. He raised the gun, aimed it directly at Ben's head. When he spoke, all traces of humour had vanished. His voice was as hard as the metal in his mouth.

'Do we have a deal?'

⚊ GOLD TEETH ⚊

Ben had never seen Truby angry. He understood that fact only now, watching him struggle to contain the emotion. Truby appeared calm, but Ben saw his eyes burn with a cold, implacable rage. One corner of his mouth twitched; the only visible sign that Truby was agitated.

All around them, the jungle hummed. It seemed alive and malevolent, impenetrable and merciless. Ben's T-shirt stuck to his back and chest. Drops of sweat rolled down the side of his face. The taste of salt was on his lips. The seconds seemed to tick past, painfully slow.

The kidnapper slid a small backpack from his left shoulder. He tossed it across to Truby.

'Open it. There's a tablet computer inside. I got it hooked up with the internet. There's a cell phone mast not far from here. We got fast access in the jungle, how d'you like that?'

With slow deliberation, Truby removed the tablet computer from the backpack, held it between his thumb and one finger, as though it were dirty laundry.

'The internet browser is open at a gold-buying site. I know you got an account there. I'm gonna need you to tap in your user ID and password, buy twenty million in gold bars, have it shipped direct from their gold bullion storage in Zurich to a safe deposit box in the city. You'll find the address on the document I've opened up on the computer.'

Truby folded his arms, tucked the computer to his chest. Ben eyed him anxiously. It didn't look as though Truby was going to comply.

'Where's Richie?'

For a moment the kidnapper seemed confused. 'Oh – that the other kid's name?'

Truby held the kidnapper's gaze. 'You know it is.'

'Uh-uh.' A shake of his head. 'I just watched you, your neighbour, I saw he had a kid. Figured you'd be the neighbourly type. Glad to see I was right.'

Once again, the flash of gold teeth.

'Listen carefully. I can give you money. But I want to see Richie. Now.'

Gold Teeth frowned. 'That ain't gonna happen.'

'Touch him,' Truby said in a voice that dripped with menace, 'and I'll do my best to kill you. Maybe you'll kill me first; we'll see. But either way, you won't get your gold.'

Ben watched the kidnapper. The man was trying to smile, but his heart wasn't in it.

'You think I believe . . . ?' Gold Teeth began.

But Truby interrupted, 'I want to see Richie. I need him here, right in front of me, before I give you so much as a sliver of gold leaf. You'd better have him somewhere close. Or this could get quite complicated.'

Gold Teeth shook his head, still smiling. 'I got him close by, Jason Truby, don't you worry about that. He's a little ways past the clearing over in the woods, back there. You send your boy to fetch him, you and me, we wait here. They don't come back in ten minutes, I cut off your left hand with the machete. Fifteen, I take one of your ears. Twenty, I take the other ear. Twenty-five . . .'

'And you take something else, yeah yeah; we get it,' snapped Truby. 'Ben's not going to try to escape.'

'Damn straight he isn't. Without a machete to cut a path, the only way out of this jungle sweat-box is this trail, right here.'

The kidnapper waved Ben ahead. He dashed back into the woods, to the clearing and began to hunt along the freshly-cut route through the tangle of trees.

Richie had been bound and gagged with a blue bandana, and then tied to the base of a tree. His hands were held in front of him with plastic cuffs. He wore forest-green hiking shorts and a burgundy Nike T-shirt. The teenager sat on the ground, legs outstretched, barefoot. Shoulder-length, fair hair was plastered to his head in sweaty strands. When he saw Ben his eyes lit up, but didn't altogether lose their fearful expression.

Ben untied the cords that bound Richie to the tree. He removed the gag.

'I don't have anything to cut through the cuffs,' Ben began, apologetic. 'And I'm sorry you don't have any shoes. But we've got to move fast. Can you do that?'

Richie nodded, eyes wide. He was smaller and

skinnier than Ben, and although they were the same age, Richie looked like a little boy; exhausted and terrified.

Ben tried to smile. He put a hand on the boy's shoulder, the way Truby so often did to him. 'It's going to be all right.'

They were back with Truby and Gold Teeth just as the kidnapper was reaching for his machete. When he saw the boys, he put it back.

'There y'are. Knew you'd come through for me.' He cocked the pistol, aimed it at Ben once again. 'Now, Mister Truby, let's go shopping for gold.'

'Why gold?' Ben said, suddenly curious. 'Why not just have him transfer the money to your account?'

Gold Teeth gave a dangerous smile. 'I appreciate the interest in my line of work. But speak again and I really will have to teach you some manners.'

The day had already grown pretty warm and Ben was still flushed from the dash into the bush. Even so, he felt himself redden further at the man's words.

Truby was calm, but the situation was still extremely dangerous. Twenty million was a mind-boggling sum for a ransom, but even so, Ben suspected that the amount wouldn't trouble Truby. The tension that Ben sensed rising from him was about something else.

When Ben realised what it might be, he tried to swallow in a dry throat.

If this went through, only two things would link Gold Teeth to this crime: the safe deposit box in Zurich, and three witnesses.

Ben felt a strange stillness sweep through him as the inevitability of it struck him.

Gold Teeth was going to kill them all, after Truby had transferred the gold. Of course. He couldn't afford to leave witnesses.

'What's the delay?' Gold Teeth snarled at Truby. 'Get on with it. You might want to sit down.'

Still Truby made no move to obey. He simply continued to regard their kidnapper 'Let the boys sit in the helicopter.'

Gold Teeth looked surprised.

'I'd like some reassurance that you aren't going to let loose with the bullets once we're done here,' Truby said with a sigh. 'Putting the boys out of harm's way is going to make it easier for me to transfer this gold.'

The kidnapper continued to stare at Truby, incredulous. He curled his left hand towards the helicopter. 'You think I can't get to them in the helicopter? They can lock themselves in there – I'll shoot through the walls. I'll blow up the goddamn gas tank and cook 'em inside. You gonna have to trust me, Truby, 'cause you got nothing else. Now, start transferring or I start chopping.' His eyes went to Richie. 'We'll start with him. I'll get real imaginative with you, boys.'

'OK, OK,' Truby said. 'I'll do it. But only when the boys are in the helicopter. Use that machete and you'll have to drop your guard. There's still two more of us than of you.'

For a moment, they all held their breath.

'Get inside,' ordered Gold Teeth, eventually. He waved Ben and Richie ahead, then turned the gun on Truby. 'Start the transfer. I'm getting tired of playing the nice guy.'

Ben was numb with disbelief as he led Richie, still in cuffs, to the helicopter. They'd walked past Truby, left him behind at least five metres away, when Ben heard him say to Gold Teeth, 'So tell me, what kind of *scuzzball* is your boss, using a man's neighbourliness to rob him?'

The word had been unmistakeable. Ben felt his pulse speed up.

Scuzzball. The go-word.

Get the heck out of Dodge, without a glance at what you leave behind.

They reached the Sikorsky. Opening the door for Richie, Ben gazed back at Truby, over thirty metres away now. He sat cross-legged on the hiking trail, tapping at the tablet computer in his lap.

Dread rose within Ben. His hand trembled slightly as he fumbled with the opposite passenger door, opening it on the side that couldn't be seen from Gold Teeth's position. Ignoring Richie's gasp, Ben transferred into the pilot seat of the cockpit.

Scuzzball. There could be no doubt. Truby had issued the go-order. Ben had to leave. He wasn't allowed to think about what might happen to Truby.

Truby knew exactly what Gold Teeth intended to do, once the instruction to ship the gold had gone through. He was trying to save Ben and Richie.

All the sweat on Ben's body seemed to freeze as the air-conditioning kicked in. He reached for the helicopter's battery switch, rolled the throttle to idle.

It's an order, he told himself. Truby's order. *I can't disobey*.

Ben tightened his left hand around the collective and prepared to lift the helicopter.

So why did he feel like a cold-hearted coward?

CANOPY

Through the partition, Ben could just hear Richie's cries of disbelief. If he'd been more relaxed, Ben would have relished giving anyone that kind of surprise.

That's right – I'm flying the Sikorsky. Get over it.

The way things were, Ben couldn't risk more than a millisecond of mind-space for anything other than flying the helicopter. How could he follow Truby's order? He'd have to shut down some part of himself – the part that wanted to save Truby.

Ben wasn't sure he could do that. Not at all.

He leaned on the cyclic, pushed forwards. The landing skids lifted off the ground. He began to twist the heli, no more than ten metres in the air. Then he was facing Gold Teeth and Jason Truby through the windscreen. The Sikorsky hovered; a giant insect preparing to strike.

The kidnapper stared back, mouth open in a furious snarl. His hands moved swiftly to holster the handgun. He swung the rifle up onto his shoulder.

Fear coursed through Ben as he realised what Gold Teeth was going to do. That rifle was deadly accurate. He'd only need to get a couple of rounds off to take out some vital system of the Sikorsky.

Ben's knuckles tightened on the throttle.

The first shot rang out, ricocheted off the rotor blade. It was enough to make the helicopter judder. In the time it took Ben to blink, Gold Teeth had reloaded the rifle and was going for a second shot.

Ben was ready to take the S-76 higher when from behind Gold Teeth, he saw Truby move. Truby threw aside the tablet computer, leapt to his feet. He dashed forward, one arm outstretched.

Truby was going for Gold Teeth's pistol. He'd put one hand on it when Gold Teeth swung round, knocking Truby to the ground. Then Truby was flat on his back, both hands clutching the gun. Gold Teeth stood no more than two metres away, legs apart, rifle pointing down.

Both were aiming straight at each other's heads.

Ben's muscles seemed to have seized up. He willed himself to raise the collective, make the helicopter lift higher.

Get the heck out of Dodge.

The low thrum of the rotor blades pounded in time with his heart. Ben inhaled, once.

Time to move.

The helicopter dipped, headed directly for the two men on the ground. Gold Teeth loomed large in the windscreen, barely a metre away. At the last instant, Ben pulled the cyclic to the left. The heli swung around. The landing skids scraped past the kidnapper.

A shot went off. Ben saw the rifle fly into the air. In the corner of the windscreen, he caught a glimpse of

Gold Teeth on the ground, struggling with Truby.

The helicopter's momentum kept swinging it around. He'd totally misjudged the manoeuvre. The aircraft had gone into a spin, barely two metres above the ground. Panic raced along his nerves as Ben tried to get the machine back under control. The simulator version of the Sikorsky S-76 would have stabilised by now, he was certain. Frustrated, Ben watched Truby swing into view for a third time.

This time, Truby was alone. On his back, leaning on his elbows, staring up at Ben behind the windscreen. No sign of Gold Teeth. No sign of the gun.

Truby looked absolutely aghast.

In Truby's eyes, Ben had his answer. Gold Teeth must have grabbed hold of the landing skids. He was throwing the entire weight calculation off. None of Ben's simulator exercises could help him now. Every single impulse he'd practised was irrelevant. An extra ninety kilos was hanging from the landing skids, shifting its position all the time.

Even an experienced pilot would have found it hard to fly well under these conditions.

A shudder hit Ben, a blast of pure fear. Death by helicopter. Broken bones, shards of glass piercing him everywhere, flames roaring, consuming the flesh. Heat and agony.

A death that might be only seconds away.

He released the pent-up breath. He tugged at the collective, lifting the craft high into the air. The spinning motion slowed. In the next few seconds, Ben was able to get some grip on his bearings.

The helicopter was hovering about twenty metres in the air. It was well above the canopy of the trees, which rarely reached more than five metres off the ground. He felt the pull of extra weight move to the pilot-side of the helicopter. With a slight flick of his wrist on the cyclic, Ben adjusted. He overcompensated; the helicopter lurched violently to the left.

For one terrifying second, the entire field of view from the co-pilot's side filled up with the ground beneath them – a carpet of countless greens; the canopy.

He'd lost sight of Truby, lost most sense of direction. In the passenger cabin, Richie was screaming. *What the hell is going on, man? Do you even know how to fly this freakin' machine? Put me back on the ground, you maniac, you're going to kill us all!*

When Ben thought about the extra weight, his mind became sunk in calculations, extra mass, vectors of forces, degrees of compensation.

Be the helicopter. Feel it as an extension of you.

Ben closed his eyes for a split second, allowing the sensation of swinging in the air to pass through his body. To let his muscles and bones make the calculations, not his head. When he opened his eyes again, the helicopter was level, flying in a straight line over the trees, the blue line of the Caribbean stretching wide in front of him.

Then Gold Teeth's face was right in front of Ben's, sneering at him through the glass. The helicopter door began to open. Desperately, Ben grabbed the handle, held it shut. With his left hand, Gold Teeth lifted a pistol to the screen. It was less than a metre from Ben's face. The man's lips pulled wide across the golden grille, a humourless grin.

He fired twice.

A cloud of glass powder burst free of the windscreen. Ben flinched, violently. His guts lurched as the signal from his brain insisted: *you're going to die.*

Then he was staring at two whitened patches on the windscreen. The bullets hadn't gone through. Still the crazy kidnapper held on to the outside of the helicopter. He seemed bent on emptying the entire magazine into the windscreen. Bullet by bullet, it was being reduced to crumbling powder.

Even above the rotor blade, Ben could hear Gold Teeth's roar of frustration. But as suddenly as he'd appeared on the pilot side of the windscreen, the kidnapper disappeared.

Ben felt weight shift from the right to the left. For a second or two, he allowed himself to stay calm. Those bullets wouldn't be any more effective on that side. The entire windscreen was bullet-proof.

Then Ben realised – he wouldn't be able to protect the door on the other side.

His reaction was almost instantaneous – a plan B that he'd only dared to contemplate. He didn't want to kill anyone. But it was starting to look like life or death.

The Sikorsky swooped low to the trees. The second

that Ben felt the landing skids hit the canopy, he pulled the aircraft level.

The yelling began. At first it sounded like rage. The sounds soon turned to muffled screams of pain. Ben could feel the helicopter being buffeted with every blow. He tried not to think about what it must feel like to be dragged through the trees. But he had to shake off Gold Teeth. If the kidnapper managed to climb inside the helicopter, Ben, Truby and Richie were all as good as dead. He circled around, lifting the skids above the canopy for a few seconds. It must have felt like a blessed reprieve. But it didn't last long.

'This time, just jump off, idiot,' Ben hissed under his breath.

He pushed forward on the cyclic. The blurry sea of green swam into view once again, the leaves coming into sharper definition as the heli descended.

There were two more heavy thwacks. And then, like a magic spell, the helicopter felt suddenly light as a feather. Ben soared along with the machine. He turned the Sikorsky back, flew low until he'd spotted Gold Teeth. The kidnapper was clinging, desperate, arms and legs wrapped around the high branch of a tree.

Ben had beaten Gold Teeth. He'd done it – alone.

Ben circled for a few moments. His eyes scoured the ground, hunting for the trail. He might never have found it. But Truby made a fire. After fifteen minutes a thread of white smoke rose from the green leaves he'd thrown on top of the flames.

Five minutes later, Ben was sweating again.

Landing a helicopter was something he'd never done in real life. Not alone, not with a teacher beside him. *Never.* The idea of it was enough to make him tremble.

For once, something in his life turned out to be as easy as the simulator. No storm, no rain, no ninety-kilo psychopath hanging from the landing skids.

Once in a while, things worked out.

After he'd landed the vehicle, Ben opened the door to the helicopter's pilot seat. He moved across to the co-pilot position. Moments later, Truby appeared at the door. His face was dark, thunderous.

Ben's spirits plummeted. *No way! He's angry?*

Wordlessly, Truby took the flight controls. Ben thought he heard the passenger door. He opened his mouth to say so.

'Don't talk,' Truby warned. 'Don't say a word or so help me, Ben, I'm liable to lose it.'

The passenger door to the rear had definitely been slid into the open position. Ben craned his neck just in time to see Richie disappearing along the trail, back into the thicket.

Ben stared at Truby. He pointed towards the passenger section and shrugged. As if to say 'what the heck?'

Truby gave a dismissive shake of his head. 'Someone will come for the kid, don't worry about it.'

'Is . . . is it OK to leave him here though?'

'You think I'm going to help someone who helped fleece me to the tune of twenty million?'

Ben was open-mouthed. 'You think . . . Richie and your neighbour were in on this too?'

Truby just stared ahead, his mouth a hard, straight line. After a long moment he said, 'Who else.' It wasn't a question. Then; 'I told Mario Torres that I had an account with that gold bullion exchange in Zurich.'

'But Mario must know he'd be a suspect.'

'He's probably not even in the country, by now,' Truby growled. 'Twenty million, that's ten apiece for him and the kidnapper. Enough money that he can hide away from the law.' With sudden violence, he slammed a hand against the side of the helicopter, emitting a sound of incoherent rage. 'To use his own boy!'

Ben stayed still and silent. He knew how such a betrayal of trust must feel. His own father and another executive had deceived most of the board of Carrington International. It had led to the complete bankruptcy of the company, as well as his mother's own rescue agency, the Caroliners.

'And you,' Truby said, turning to Ben. He still looked furious. 'Do you even know how to take an order, Benedict? You almost got yourself killed. And that other kid, too.'

Ben lowered his eyes a little, but said, in an even voice, 'You may as well know it; I can't leave my friends to die. Not if I can do *anything*.'

Truby seemed genuinely disarmed by the response. Ben could see the man's anger in the white-knuckled grip of his fist on the cyclic. But to his surprise, there was no follow-up.

'At least he didn't manage to rip you off,' Ben said, hopefully.

The flare of wrath in Truby's expression told Ben exactly how far off the mark that comment was. 'The transaction went through. Twenty million,' Truby muttered. He sounded appalled.

'Why *gold*?'

'Gold is the ultimate transferable resource,' Truby said. 'Some people, they'll do anything to get their hands on it. Lie to friends, cheat their partners, kill . . . Oh, most definitely, they'll kill.'

His eyes looked haunted. 'We were lucky today, Ben.'

— GAME —

'Word is, you did some significant badass-ery out there on Cozumel.' Addison faced Ben with a challenging grin as she set down a mug of hot tea on the side table next to the sofa. 'English breakfast, right?'

Ben picked up the mug. Truby had flown them home *'just in time for afternoon tea'*. 'Builder's tea, yeah, thanks, Addi.'

Addison waited. She looked as though she might be ready to wait all day. 'So . . .' she prompted, gently. 'The badass-ery?'

Ben stalled, the hot tea halfway to his lips. 'I'm afraid I don't know what you mean.'

'Give it up, Carrington.' Her smile turned wicked. 'You *did* something. Dietz knows. He's obviously sworn to secrecy.'

'Far be it from me to go against Jason Truby's rules.' But coming from Ben, those words sounded hollow, even to himself. He gave Addison a thoughtful glance, dying to tell her what had happened on Cozumel.

I'm going to have a good, long think about what happened here, Ben. It's not that I don't see your point. No one wants to let their friends suffer. But some organisations have to rely on a chain of command. Not just the military – anything where lives are at stake. You're sixteen, dammit. Got your whole life ahead of you. Don't be so eager to throw it away.

'Where's Jasmine?' Ben said, changing the subject. 'And Rigel?'

'Actually, they're together. She took him for a walk around the lower decks. There's more space there.'

'Only if you count the stairs,' Ben said doubtfully. Or maybe there were decks even lower than the ones he'd seen so far? He made a mental note to ask Dietz for a proper tour of 'engineering'.

In fact, Jasmine had finished walking Rigel. When the lift opened on the other side of the deck to the living area, Ben watched her emerge with the dog padding contentedly at her side. He stood up, ready to go over and greet her.

But Denny beat him to it. He must have been lurking on the opposite side of the central conference area, and emerged with a plate in each hand. Ben sat down again. The trio were on their way over to him and Addison.

Jasmine and Denny sat on the two-seater sofa opposite the larger couch on which Ben and Addison were lounging. It wasn't entirely clear whether they intended to include the others in their conversation, which seemed to have started sometime earlier that morning.

'I saw that photo of you that Jonah posted online. You see how many comments it's had?' Denny was saying.

Jasmine blushed. 'I told him not to post pictures of me.'

Denny flashed a charming smile. 'A man's gotta let other dudes know how cute his girl is.' Before she could object, he raised a quick eyebrow. 'How's your sandwich?'

Jasmine took a bite. After a moment she was nodding her appreciation. 'Wow.'

'Hand-sliced corned beef and potato salad on rye,' Denny said. 'All from Zabar's. I brought a personal supply. Don't think I could live anywhere but Manhattan now. I'm like, addicted.'

Ben placed his mug of tea on the nearby table. He forced himself to push aside his irritation at Denny's obvious attempts to flirt with Jasmine. He pretended instead to be paying attention to Rigel, patting the dog's head and caressing him behind the ears, all the while listening to what was being said not two metres away.

'You should consider Columbia,' Denny continued, 'You know, for college. You go to an international school, right? American strand or French?'

Jasmine said, 'French.'

'That's cool, so you'll be doing the International Baccalaureate? You can get into US colleges with that.'

'I don't know,' she replied.

Ben bent his head to whisper 'good dog' into Rigel's ear. It was a handy way to shield his eyes from Jasmine and Denny.

'I like Switzerland,' Jasmine said. 'I'm kind of a home-girl. I like to be near my mom.'

'Oh, I understand,' Denny said, with such exaggerated confidence that Ben strongly doubted that he did.

'And I guess you're worried about leaving Jonah too,' Denny said casually. He made it sound oh-so-innocent. Like he was asking about the weather forecast.

'Jonah?' Jasmine shook her head, firmly. 'That's an awful long time to be planning ahead.'

'How long have you guys been going together?'

Addison dipped her head in an almost imperceptible nod at Ben. Still shielded behind Rigel, Ben acknowledged her silent comment with a secretive smile.

'A year and five months,' Jasmine said, after a moment's thought.

Denny sighed. 'That's a long-term relationship, by my calculations.'

'What – you've never had a girlfriend for that long?'

Another sigh. 'I haven't even gone steady.'

This time, Ben couldn't contain a scornful laugh.

Denny turned to him, as though he hadn't been aware all along of his audience. 'What's your deal?'

'You've never had a girlfriend? That's not what you told me.'

'Did I say "girlfriend"? I said I hadn't *gone steady*.' Denny turned soft brown eyes on Jasmine. 'I'm looking for someone real special. So far, no luck. All the best ones are taken.'

'Oh, please,' snorted Ben.

'What about you, Mister I'm-too-busy-for-a-girlfriend?'

'Never said that.'

Denny smirked.

'Oh, that's right,' he said. 'You're Mister I'm-so-mature-I-should-be-with-an-older-woman.'

Ben's mouth fell open. 'What . . .?'

This time, everyone heard Addison's reaction – a short, sharp laugh.

'Hey, back me up on this, why don't you?' said Denny, turning to Addison. 'You've heard Ben say he likes Lola, right?'

Addison passed a hand over her mouth, as if to conceal a laugh. 'Maybe,' she conceded.

'You're being a total prat,' Ben said, angrily. 'That's literally the worst attempt to hit on someone else's girlfriend that I've ever seen.'

'What's your technique, Romeo?' countered Denny. 'Do share.'

Lightly, Jasmine said, 'You think I don't know when I'm being hit on?' She gave both boys a fake-sweet smile. 'Ben – thanks but I *so* don't need your protection. Denny – you can keep trying, but I'm not going to break up with Jonah so that I can date you.'

'Break up with him?' Denny said. 'Not even necessary. Jonah is all the way over in Switzerland. You and me – we're here.'

'Nice,' said Ben, his voice dripping sarcasm. 'Very smooth.'

'It often pays to be direct,' Denny said, pointedly. 'But I can guess the approach a guy like you would prefer. Oooh, Jasmine, let me protect you, let me shield you from the cold, let me save you.'

'A guy like me . . . ?' Ben began, angrily.

Jasmine stood up, shaking her head. She looked from one boy to the other, disappointment filling her eyes. 'Seriously?' She stepped forward and without asking Ben's permission, took hold of Rigel's collar. 'Come on, boy. Let's do another circuit.'

Then she was gone. Denny sat back down with the rest of his sandwich, munching happily, as though nothing had happened.

Ben too resumed his seat. He turned to Addison, ashen-faced. 'What just happened?'

'Y'all got burned, is what.' Addison glared at Denny. He returned her stare, eyes twinkling. 'Think you're something of a player, don't you?' she asked him.

'I got game,' he said, calmly. 'If that makes me a "player" then, all right.'

'"Game" is not going to work,' Addison advised. 'Not with Jasmine.'

Denny just smiled, shaking his head as his eyes lowered. 'No offence, Addi, but you're not the type this works on.'

'You think Jasmine is?'

Denny didn't answer right away. 'We'll see,' was all he eventually said.

Ben was quiet through their entire exchange. It was

quite an accusation to have levelled at him, that he played the hero to impress girls. Was that what people thought Ben had been trying to do with Jasmine?

Was that what *Jasmine* thought?

'You flew the Sikorsky?' Denny's question felt like the start of an interrogation.

Ben nodded. 'You know I did. I told you – Jason took me out for a lesson.'

'But he helped, yes? With the take-off and landing? I mean, Truby dual-controlled you, right?'

The truth was that Ben had ended up doing both those things without any help whatsoever. They hadn't been done all that elegantly, but he'd made it into the air and onto the ground in one piece. This was more than he could tell Denny.

Truby couldn't have been clearer – *You had a normal first lesson, OK? Don't go around boasting about solo-flying or anything.*

'It was a perfectly standard lesson,' Ben told Denny. He bit his lower lip, then added, 'I wasn't especially good.'

Denny seemed to eat this up. 'Why would you be? I mean, have you shown any particular aptitude for flight?'

Ben frowned. 'Like what?'

'Like, d'you ever take the PILAPT test? It's an aptitude test. Most recruiters use it for the air forces.'

'No, I haven't,' Ben said.

When he saw Denny's delighted grin, Ben began to wonder if he'd walked into a trap.

'I have an idea,' Denny said. 'Why don't we both take it, right now? We can do a prep test online.'

Addison was still sitting in the general vicinity, looking at the e-reader in her hand. She looked up as their conversation touched on the PILAPT test.

'You should do a prep test,' she agreed. 'Kind of surprised that Truby hasn't made you do one already.'

Denny stood. 'Let's go. The loser buys dinner at a swanky restaurant, deal?'

'What "swanky restaurant"?' Ben asked. 'In case you hadn't noticed, we're about sixty kilometres from the nearest coast.'

'You'll visit New York City, some day. When you do, if you beat my score today, dinner's on me.'

'No,' Ben said, as an idea struck him. 'If I win, you promise to leave Jasmine alone. Stop hitting on her.'

A slow smile crawled across Denny's face. 'Ah. You wanna play for a girl.' He punched Ben's arm, a little too hard to be friendly. 'Way to go, dude. I underestimated you.'

Addison folded her arms across her chest. 'Really, Ben? You want to play "who's the bigger idiot" with *this* guy?'

Ben didn't take his eyes from Denny's. 'No – I didn't mean it like that. I just want you to let her be.'

'Oho, so you don't want the way clear for yourself?'

'Hey,' objected Ben, 'Jasmine *has* a boyfriend.'

'You British – so polite! She won't thank you for it. Trust me on this, Ben, if you like Jasmine you should make a move. Boyfriend or not.'

Ben said, firmly, 'Do we have a deal?'

Addison gave a resigned shake of her head. 'Jasmine better not find out about this, is all I'm saying.'

A little apprehensive, Ben followed Denny to the command centre, where most of the workstations stood empty. Denny sat down in one of the seats, waited as a laptop rose from the mechanised arm that had been tucked away on the right hand side. Ben picked a station on the other side of the command centre, still facing the panel of high-definition TV screens. He activated the laptop in the arm of the seat. He felt for the headset in the button-activated drawer just under the chair. Addison disappeared for a second and returned with two joysticks that each boy plugged into his computer.

A few seconds later they were ready, headsets in place, hands on joysticks, the relevant test located on the internet. Addison started a stopwatch, pumped the display up to one of the large HDTV screens.

'OK,' she said. 'Start the test.'

The pilot aptitude test was a combination of numerical reasoning, reaction time and hand-eye coordination tests that made use of the joystick. Ben felt that he'd done pretty well on the hand-eye coordination at least. He'd discovered as a young boy that hand-eye coordination skills were transferrable between most ball games. Ben had been the captain of the Under-16 lacrosse team at Kenton College. It didn't come as such a surprise to him therefore, that he found this part of the test easy.

He couldn't say the same of the numerical reasoning, however.

When their time was up, Addison put both scores on the board. Alongside was a list of the pass mark required for different air forces as well as commercial airlines.

Denny's score was six points higher.

'You'd get into a bunch of air forces, Denny, and most of the commercial airlines too, including Qantas. Which is pretty hardcore,' said Addison, the admiration evident in her voice. 'Ben, you'd get into some of them too.'

'But not Qantas,' Ben groaned.

'Focus on the positive. You'd *both* be considered as pilot material. And Gemini Force isn't Qantas.'

Ben pushed the laptop aside in anger. 'Gemini Force should be way tougher to get into than Qantas.'

How could that smarmy drip have beaten him?

Denny seemed to make a point of putting his laptop away with immense care and precision. He stood, one hand stretched out to Ben.

'Well played, "old bean".'

Reluctantly, Ben returned the handshake. 'Fair enough. OK, what's the fanciest restaurant in New York?'

Eyes wide with innocence, Denny said, 'I guess that would be the Manhattan Marineville. But we didn't play for dinner. Remember?' He mouthed, silently, the word 'Jasmine'.

Ben turned pale. There was nothing he could say – it had been his own idea. His eyes flickered for an instant as he noticed Addison's fingers moving in a rhythmic pattern against the desk. When she repeated the motion, he focused. She was using the secret Gemini Force hand signals to tap out *'Don't be an ass.'*

'Quit looking so worried,' Denny commented, apparently oblivious to the message from Addison. 'Nothing's changed, really.'

Somehow, Ben doubted that. By drawing attention to Denny hitting on Jasmine, he'd made a thing of it. Maybe it really had just been a bit of fun for Denny. Now Ben had turned it into something bigger – a way for Denny to prove something to Ben.

Denny gave one of his trademark smirks and then made some excuse about having to catch up on some reading for his differential equations class. Ben waited around for Addison to finish collecting up the joysticks. He followed her to the equipment cupboard in the central, circular units that surrounded the conference room.

'You think I'm being stupid,' he volunteered.

Addison didn't respond immediately.

'Well?' Ben's hands balled into tense fists. 'Let's have it.'

She turned to him with an inscrutable smile. 'You don't see what he's doing?'

'No, what?'

'Saw a lot of this in the air force. Guys trying to out-alpha each other. He's trying to be Top Gun, Ben.' She shook her head, gently placed a hand on his arm. 'Don't get sucked in. You're with Gemini Force and Denny isn't. My money says he's tried that PILAPT test before. And anyhow, aptitude is only part of what's important.'

'Qantas don't seem to think so,' Ben muttered.

'*Qantas* isn't running a rescue agency. What counts in Gemini Force, above aptitude, above skills and knowledge, is *heart*. We don't go the extra mile because we're trying to win a battle for a general or score customer service points. We're counting every single person we can save. They're all special. And that takes heart.' She tapped him lightly on the chest and grinned. 'You got bags of heart, don't you, Ben?'

Ben couldn't answer right away.

'Hopefully more of it than that Denny creep.'

'Don't be too hard on the kid,' she said. 'He's been coming here to visit his mom since Gemini Force got started. Now he finds you're the new golden boy in town. Denny's the kind of guy who rises to that kind of bait. Doesn't mean you have to.'

Unsteadily Ben said, 'I should – what – be the better man?'

'Be the *man*,' she said with a short laugh. 'And not the horny teenager.'

Ben risked a shy grin. 'I'm only flesh and blood. And Lola is gorgeous.'

'You and Lola?' Addison snorted. 'Yeah, right. Your crush on Lola - that's why you're so eager to protect *Jasmine*.'

— KRAV MAGA —

At seven the next morning they took their places in the gym, Ben, James, Toru, Tim, Paul and Addison, all dressed in identical GF One gym outfits – grey cargo trousers and T-shirts. As he moved through some simple stretching exercises, Ben remembered the first *krav maga* lesson he'd taken.

His mother Caroline had been alive, back then. She and Addison had just been invited to join Gemini Force. Not Ben. He'd been a mere spectator. That *krav maga* lesson, like every other interaction he'd had with Truby and the crew of GF One, had been an opportunity to show what Ben might be able to do – if they'd just teach him and trust him.

'I've given this a lot of thought,' Truby had announced. He'd taken his time, looked around the room slowly, connected one by one with each person in the room.

'I realise that you guys are pacifists now. Except Ben, I mean. OK – I respect your position on war. You have my word – Gemini Force will never knowingly attack anyone. We're not armed. We'll never provoke a fight. But there *will* be times when we'll encroach on someone's plans. I'm thinking mainly of terrorists. They'll stop at nothing. I won't send you into a situation like that without some protection.

'To that end, James is gonna train all the pilots in *krav maga*. It's not for wimps; that's for sure. One day though, it may save your life.'

To the general amusement of all, Jason Truby himself had spent a fair bit of the *krav maga* session flat on his back.

They'd begun with philosophy.

'*Krav maga* isn't about fighting. It's about *ending* a fight, as quickly as possible. The first thing is the mind-set. Someone's coming at you with a knife? That's raw menace, inches away from your face. From your throat. From your guts. Easy to be scared. The most understandable thing in the world, to feel like a victim. But if you do – you're going to wind up getting hurt. That's the first lesson. *Never think like a victim. Always attack.*'

James had taught them how to push back at an attacker with both hands, using all the energy and momentum that they could put behind the shove. That had been fun – seeing how far you could actually shift someone, if you seriously meant it. Ben had particularly enjoyed watching his mother shoving Truby across the gym room. He'd looked a little surprised, too. As though he wasn't even letting her do it.

Then they'd worked on the mental preparation for a fight. Once you knew someone was about to attack, James told them, you had seconds in which to do some essential prep work.

'Assess your fighting space – your *dynamic sphere*. You need to own that space – control who's inside it. Someone inside your dynamic sphere can quickly deliver a deadly blow. Keep a safe distance at all times from your opponent. Only move closer when you're going to attack.'

They'd spent most of that first lesson just shoving each other and dancing in and out of each other's dynamic spheres. James was right – you quickly learned the danger of letting a fighter get too close. All it took was a millisecond of lost focus and you'd wind up with a hard kick. Caroline's fifteen years of *aikido* training had made her a tricky opponent; slippery, evasive, neatly disengaging from holds with elegant ease, as if she were untying a climbing knot.

After that first lesson Ben had noticed, with pride, a new level of respect for Caroline; grudgingly admiring comments from all. Especially Truby, who admitted that he was well out of his comfort zone.

'I'm four parts nerd, one part jock,' Truby had said, with a mildly grumbling tone. 'And the jock part prefers something less combative.'

'Well, Benedict is more like four parts jock, one part nerd,' Caroline had laughed.

Sadness pulsed through Ben at the memory. But he accepted it, didn't push the feeling away. Wasn't that why he'd asked to stay on GF One, after all? He'd told Truby that he wanted to remember his mother in this place, above all others.

James Winch approached, the muscles of his shoulders bunching beneath his T-shirt. The guy was a haystack compared with the pilots, who all tended to lithe, slim frames rather than solid bulk. Ben identified immediately with James. He himself was built more in that mode. If he didn't have the muscle yet, it was because of his age.

'Today we're going to work more on defending from knives.'

Ben felt a tingle of happy anticipation. Knives. Scarier and more unpredictable than guns – that's what James had drummed into his colleagues in Gemini Force.

They'd spent a lot of time defending from attackers with guns. It turned out that if you moved like lightning, with purpose, determination and most of all, practice, then you could usually disarm a gunman who stepped into your dynamic sphere.

Someone who wanted to shoot you didn't need to get close. If they did get close, the gun was more often than not a last resort, or simply a threat.

'Call their bluff by going for the gun and *actually meaning it*,' James had told them. 'That's always going to take them by surprise. People who stick a gun in your face think they own you. *Use* that.'

James raised his right hand, which held a realistic-looking, hard rubber knife.

'Knife attack. Remember, it probably won't be like you've seen in films. Won't be a single swipe that you can comfortably knock away. Think more in terms of wild, unpredictable. Stabbing movements that come from any number of directions. I can teach you how to defend from most positions. But the truth is, there are a couple of attacks that are almost impossible to stop. That's why knives are so bloody dangerous. I'd rather face a guy with a gun than a knife, any day of the week.'

Ben was pleased with how he performed, overall, especially in his bout with Tim. The Scot was shorter than him by about four centimetres, with arms and shoulders that were powerful from working out with weights. Not only that but Tim was quick, light on his feet. He'd been awarded a boxing Blue at Oxford University, apparently. It showed.

Yet Ben held up well. He had tremendous upper body strength, essential for climbing. James nodded approvingly when Ben took a knife off Tim for the second time.

'All right, everyone. Let's have a think about strategy. Most opponents will just go for you. Won't be expecting much of a fight. But once in a while, you'll come up against someone who has an inkling that you might stand up to them. That's when the mind games begin.'

Mind games. Ben knew exactly what James meant. Minos Winter, the criminal they'd chased down after the Horizon Alpha platform had been sabotaged: he'd done something like that.

'An opponent gets chatty?' James began. 'You ignore his words, OK? Keep your focus on the knife.'

Ben's pulse rate increased, pleasantly. He bounced on the balls of his feet, waiting. Aimless fighting wasn't fun. But working on strategy and mind games – he liked the idea of that.

━ SUITE TRUBY ━

Passing the living area on the main deck, Truby didn't break his stride to call out to Ben, who'd just finished showering and dressing after *krav maga*.

Ben followed Truby into his cabin. It was identical to every other cabin in the corridor; a simple sleeping area, a narrow desk, two easy chairs. Where every other berth had a double bunk, Truby's room had a single bed. Perplexed, he watched Truby open what should have been the door to a tiny bathroom and toilet cubicle. Instead, there was a small lift, just big enough for two. Truby stepped inside and turned to Ben. 'Let's go.'

The lift descent took at least ten seconds. When the doors opened, Ben found himself in a room he'd never seen before. The walls were made of a highly compressed grey stone, or possibly an artificial ceramic. The bricks interlocked perfectly without any visible mortar; a twelve-sided design that fitted two extra grooves into each main side of a rectangle.

A desk dominated the space. It was topped with a layer of smooth, matt leather. Embedded into the desk was a large touch screen. The only other things on the desk were a candy-striped Mini car and its remote control.

Ben examined the walls. One contained a single, round porthole, a window to the ocean beyond, darker and deeper than any glimpsed from the main decks of GF One. On an HDTV screen, a live feed of the Earth as seen from the International Space Station. There was a dartboard on which the darts had been thrown at a cheesy birthday card. In anger? Defiance of another passing year? Or maybe it was the sender's identity that was the real target?

He didn't dare ask.

Hanging from the walls were decorations that Ben recognised as memorabilia from the Gemini mission to the asteroid, 1036 Ganymed. In one corner, a model of the Earth's moon hung from the ceiling, textured, each feature of its surface apparently to scale. He glanced at Truby, seeking permission to look more closely. Truby nodded, once. 'Go right ahead.'

Ben moved silently around the room, looking at newspaper cuttings, the blueprints of GF One and of other vehicles in the Gemini Force stable. He paused for a couple of seconds at one frame. It was an article about the tragic death of airman Jonathan Truby following his capture by the Republican Guard in Iraq.

Jason's twin brother. Tortured to death, while Jason was making his first million. Ben knew that the injustice of this, the horrific imbalance, still haunted Truby. With all his billions, he simply couldn't let himself relax, not while he remembered Jonathan.

'Some folk get to live for their wives, their husbands

and kids,' Truby said in a soft voice, standing just to Ben's left. 'And some of us are living for the ones who didn't get to finish their time.'

Ben turned to face Truby. He was grateful that at least one person on GF One understood – Ben wasn't just trying to distract himself from the loss of his parents. He doubted that he'd ever be a businessman, like his father. He had to live up to what the world had lost in his mother, Caroline.

Truby's voice altered a little; Ben heard a definite catch, as though the words pained him slightly. 'I'm not sure this is the right choice for you,' Truby said.

Ben swallowed, hard. Was this some kind of preamble to sending him away?

'When I saw your mother go scooting up that hotel to rescue those pilots, Ben, I thought I'd never meet anyone as reckless as her. Apart from Addison, of course. That woman is crazy-brave. But I've been thinking for a while that you might be the same.'

'I want to be,' Ben agreed. 'My mother – she showed me who I am.'

'Yes, I think she did.' Truby sighed. 'Now I know how my brother's Commanding Officer must have felt.'

'How'd you mean?'

'Sending brave youngsters into combat. Some who don't come back. Always wondered how you *live* with those decisions.'

Ben shook his head, vigorously. 'No. See – it's their decision. The ones who go. No one made my mum do what she did. Or your brother. You're just letting them be themselves. You've got to let me do that.' He looked Truby straight in the eye. 'Please, Jason.'

Truby slid open the only drawer in his desk, removed a framed photo of a handsome, blond, green-eyed young man in a Gemini Force uniform.

Ben knew immediately who this must be. 'Gary Lincoln?'

The first pilot that Truby had recruited. He'd died before the rescue agency was even fully operational.

Truby nodded. 'You know why I don't hang Gary's photo on my wall? Or your mother's? I can't handle the reminder, Ben. At least Jonathan's death isn't on *me*. Gary's death might be. He was driving to the airport too fast, because the crew had worked late on a rescue. Now Toru is alone. You think I don't see it in him, every day, how much he misses Gary? And now you. Bad enough that you lost your last parent. Now you want to risk your own life?'

Ben felt his eyes begin to mist with frustration and anger. He began to back away from Truby. 'No. Don't . . . don't you put this on me. I did what had to be done, Jason, or you'd probably be dead. I didn't even *think* about it. And I won't, all right? I'd have done the same for any of the crew.'

Truby nodded. He didn't seem surprised by Ben's outburst. 'Oh, I know that. All part of the plan for Gemini Force, son. I'm just a little taken aback by how . . . enthusiastically you've taken to it.'

'Maybe you should worry a bit more about yourself,' Ben said, sharply. 'One lousy neighbour and you've got the local gangsters on your back.'

'That guy who robbed me wasn't a local. I've met with the locals, Ben, do you think I'm a fool? They know who I am. We came to an arrangement a long time ago.'

'That Gold Teeth; he was, like, a chancer?'

'He was some kind of rogue agent, if that's what you mean. Who knows how he got to my neighbour. I'd like to believe that he forced him; threatened the boy's life, suggested that I'd be the one to help. More likely that the two of them worked on the plan together. You're right to assume there's a threat to me. Ben, I've been assured by the people that matter that I'm safe on Cozumel. If there's a threat, it's from outside my immediate circle.'

Just then, the touch screen on Truby's desk flared into life. Dietz's face appeared on the display. 'Jason, we're getting some interesting reports from South Africa. Do you want me to send the information directly to you? Or would you like to join us in the command centre?'

Truby strode over to the desk and touched a button. A fitting dropped out of the ceiling and lowered on a narrow metal tube until it was level with Truby's face. Ben guessed it contained a webcam.

'What kind of incident?' Truby asked.

'It's a gold mine. The Nomzamo mine – it's owned

by the Auron Corporation. Looks bad, Jason. We may be able to help.'

'We'll be up in five minutes,' confirmed Truby.

As the lift door closed behind them, Ben took one last look at Truby's secret suite. It struck him that he hadn't seen half of the quarters – at least two further doors were visible. He guessed that a bathroom lay behind one. What else? In the months that Ben had lived on GF One, he'd heard no mention of Truby having rooms in the lower decks. Dietz must have known that Truby wasn't within earshot when he contacted him via the computer network.

Ben wondered – who else knew about this private escape?

⎯ FEEDS ⎯

The global news feeds were streaming onto every screen that hung in the command centre. The full Gemini Force team was already there, as well as Denny and Jasmine. They were hovering by the door, ignored by the crew. Neither teenager seemed bold enough to take one of the seats, even though a couple were still empty.

With a twinge of pride, Ben realised that they'd left those seats empty for him and Truby. As if Ben belonged there more than either of them.

Truby took one seat immediately. His attention was already drawn to the multitude of screens. Ben couldn't help but notice the way that Denny held his chin in one hand, rapt by the swiftly moving information that trickled across the displays. There were updates pulled from all the main social networks, as well as videos and official newswire services.

'Is it always this *busy*?' Denny asked Truby.

Truby glanced up, yanked out of the moment by the boy's question. 'Busy? You mean the data? Nah. You get used to it.'

'Still,' Denny said, thoughtfully, 'there's got to be a better way.'

'Like what?'

'Well, like, right now, you're interested in the gold mine story, yes? I see that you're pulling all the relevant information out of the newsfeeds. But it doesn't have to be so random.'

Truby stared at Denny. Every ounce of his attention had become suddenly fixed on Nina's son. Ben watched for a moment, fascinated. What could Denny have said that had Truby so arrested?

'Go on, son,' Truby said, encouragingly.

Denny indicated one of the screens. 'It wouldn't be too difficult to write some code to put some intelligent search and aggregation algorithms into that.'

Truby smiled. 'Dietz has been suggesting we buy some software to do just that.'

Denny shrugged. 'Sure. Or I could take a day and write something that's perfect for your needs. Bet I could grab most of the code from open source. I could make it so that you can sort the feed alphabetically, in time order, relevance, whatever.'

Truby stopped smiling. Now he just looked mildly impressed. 'You could do that?'

For all his former swagger, Denny seemed surprised that this would impress Truby. 'Yeah, sure. It's a pretty simple task.'

'I mean – you could do that – *in a day*?'

Denny thought for a moment. His answer, when it came, was spoken without any hint of boast. 'Pretty sure.'

Truby said, fervently, 'Do it.'

For a second, Denny gazed back at Truby with a look of pure reverence and devotion. Without another word, he left.

A little uncomfortably, Ben took the empty seat next to Truby's. He didn't want to say anything about Denny's swift recruitment as a programmer for Gemini Force. Jason Truby, a Silicon Valley billionaire, had seemed impressed by Denny's proposal. That alone told Ben a great deal.

He peered at the screens, watched quietly with the rest of the team as they absorbed the information. After a few minutes, Ben spotted what Denny had seen. It *would* be much better if you could sort the information differently. Would this have occurred to Ben if Denny hadn't suggested it? Ben had to admit, reluctantly, *probably not*. Even if it had, he wouldn't have had the remotest idea of how to achieve that goal.

However much of a twerp Denny might be socially, he was obviously someone to be reckoned with on his own turf. Ben made a mental note never to underestimate him.

'It started yesterday,' James Winch said. He'd strolled over from the other end of the command centre where he'd been listening to something over his headset. 'I just had a call with the local rescue agency, MRA – Mining Rescue Africa. My former boss from Schlumberger heads up a team there.'

Truby looked up, sharply. 'You're not talking to Nomzamo directly?'

'Nomzamo aren't talking to *anyone* directly. The company that owns the gold mine – Auron Corporation – is dealing with the incident. And no, they won't talk to us. They want MRA to handle everything. They brought them in on the rescue yesterday, at fifteen-thirty hundred hours.'

Ben said, 'What was it? An explosion?'

As well as studying the manuals for Gemini Force's vehicles, Ben had also taken some time to learn about the history of disasters. He'd paid particular attention to any disasters that happened in mountains. This often included mining accidents.

Mostly, he'd read about accidents that happened in coal mines. The volatile combination of hydrocarbon gases and heat had too often caused explosions that not only trapped miners but also burned and poisoned them too.

So far, Ben hadn't read anything about gold mining disasters.

'It seems to be a lift malfunction,' James said. 'In the second lift shaft. It's blocked the entire lift. No one can get in or out, beyond the first shaft.'

'How far down are they trapped?' Ben asked.

'Nomzamo is one of the deepest mines in the world; three and a half kilometres deep. Three lift shafts, each a kilometre deep, take a stack of three crates down to the bottom. Each crate holds about forty miners. The lift isn't lowered – it free-falls for most of that distance. You can barely imagine the sensation,' he said, and for a brief moment, he smiled. 'Heavy equipment is fixed to the underside of the lift. Seems in this case, a railcar came loose. It tumbled down the shaft, got trapped across. The mining carriage crashed into it.' He paused, eyes flickered briefly towards Ben. 'There are . . . casualties. Now there's no way into the mine, beyond the second shaft. Which means that most of the guys in the mine below that lift shaft are trapped.

'Now, if the mine weren't so deep, this wouldn't automatically be a nightmare situation. Down there, though, the rock face is around sixty degrees centigrade. The mine has a cooling plant, underground reservoirs of ice slush. They pump cold air down there. But that only keeps the temperature at thirty five degrees. You can't take that, as well as humidity, for too long. Pretty soon heat exhaustion sets in.'

James paused. 'Then, well, you're finished. No energy to get out of there, even if you had enough water to keep your hydration levels up.'

'What's the plan, James?' asked Truby. 'What are MRA doing?'

'They're taking equipment down the first shaft, the one that's working fine. They're going to pull out the second lift and the survivors of the crash, and evacuate all the miners that are trapped above the second level. Then they're going to send a team down there to free the trapped railcar, winch it back up the shaft, then get the lift running back down again.'

Truby gestured at the screens. 'If that's true, then all this, *"hundreds of miners trapped in the world's deepest hole – closest thing to hell on earth"* – sounds like it's going to be over in twenty-four hours or so, wouldn't you say?'

James nodded.

Ben said, 'There's nothing for Gemini Force to do, is that what you're saying?'

'On the contrary,' James said, emphatically. 'We should get a team out there.'

Truby shifted in his seat. He regarded James with slow curiosity. 'Why, James?'

'It's actually not my idea. My contact at MRA suggested it.'

'Do MRA need help?'

'She told me that Auron specifically forbade them to work with any other rescue agency.'

Truby said, 'Maybe they're worried they won't be able to do it, and they want us on standby. Surely Auron will ask for help if it comes to that?'

Ben interjected, 'But why wouldn't they want another rescue agency there in the first place? Sounds a bit fishy.'

James flashed Ben a rare grin. 'The lad's got a point. There was something strange about the way my contact at MRA told me about this. I got the impression she really, really wanted us there. But she wouldn't come straight out and say it.'

'Let me get this straight,' Truby said. 'Your ex-boss, who now works at MRA, wants us on standby, but the Auron Corporation would never let us get involved?'

'Sounds like maybe there's something your ex-boss isn't telling you,' suggested Ben.

James gave Ben a faint smile. 'I had exactly the same reaction.' He turned to Truby. 'Could you spare a team? It's shaping up to be the biggest gold mining disaster for a decade. If they don't start pulling those guys out of there within twenty-four hours, I can't see how they'll live.'

'There's presumably no way to drill fast through that much rock?' Truby said.

'There may be a way to drill faster than it's been done before,' conceded James. 'But to drill *two kilometres* in a day?' He shook his head, eyes heavy with doubt. 'That's impossible. We'd have to find some other way.'

Ben held his breath as he waited for Truby's decision. A gold mine in Africa. The idea of being *kilometres* under the surface of the earth. Buried, unimaginably deep. Once down there, there'd be no way to get out quickly. You'd have to simply accept the horror of all those millions of tons of rock right over your head. Whatever claustrophobia Ben had experienced inside the mountain with Jasmine and Rigel, this would be a thousand times worse.

For once, Ben wasn't at all sure he wanted any part of the mission. Yet if Truby was prepared to risk Ben on the team . . .

It would mean that Truby had forgiven Ben's reckless disobedience on Cozumel. It would mean that Truby was coming to terms with Ben *truly* being part of Gemini Force.

━ GANYMEDIAN ━

'Briefing in the conference room. I want the whole team on standby.' Almost as if it was an afterthought, Truby said to Ben, 'You too. Grab a uniform from the storage closet. Spares are in the one by the exit to GF Two.'

The lightness of Truby's tone felt like an attempt to mask the significance of his words. Even so, to Ben each word fell like a hammer that set his heart pounding to a new and exhilarating rhythm. His stroll across the deck to the store cupboard felt more like a glide. He started to rifle through the shelves and hangers, searching for the size labels, his hands trembling, just slightly.

It's really going to happen. So why was he shaking? Was he afraid? Yes, a little, definitely. Afraid to fail, to let people down. All those expectations. But more than that, Ben was excited. In just a few moments he'd be standing alongside the rest of Gemini Force, indistinguishable from any of them.

'Too bad you don't have a call sign,' Denny said over his shoulder, making him jump. 'Still, I guess *observing* is better than nothing.' He picked out one of the microfibre grey T-shirts. 'Here. You look like a size thirty-six.'

Ben ignored the implied jibe and picked up a size forty. With the same hand he selected a pair of salopettes and with the other, a pair of boots. He elbowed aside the hangers. There didn't appear to be any jackets.

Denny noticed it too. 'Guess he just wants you in the generic grey. Better that way, so you don't stand out.'

The two boys' eyes met. Ben answered Denny's faint smugness with a defiant glare. But he managed to hold his tongue.

When Ben returned from changing in his cabin, the rest of the crew was gathered in the conference room. Everyone except Denny and Jasmine had taken a seat at the symbol of their personal call sign. In fact, he realised that the two other teenagers weren't anywhere to be seen.

Huh. Looks like I'm finally in the inner circle.

As always, the same two symbols were left vacant – Taurus and Aries. Once in a while Ben had been invited to sit at the conference table. Truby would wave a hand at the vacant positions and Ben would choose one, apparently at random. In fact, he took care to vary it – sometimes Aries, sometimes his mother's call sign, Taurus.

Ben wasn't sure why he did this. He didn't know how people had chosen their zodiac signs, or whether Truby had assigned them. The team weren't selecting based on their birthdays; Truby himself was Gemini, yet his birthday fell in September.

But then, Truby's obsession with 'Gemini' was for an entirely different reason.

Maybe it was for someone else to decide? After all, didn't astrology supposedly say something about you? Ben's star sign was Cancer – the crab. That call sign was already taken by James Winch. It fitted him well, the powerful claws of a crab were a perfect analogy for all the grabbing, digging, pulling technology that James commanded.

'Ben, siddown.' Truby looked up, expectant yet patient.

Ben suddenly felt everyone's eyes on him. They were watching to see which symbol he chose. Only then did he understand. Now that he was in uniform, this decision mattered.

He studied both signs, carved in cherry wood inlaid within the paler beech of the table. Aries. Something new; fresh. No one in Gemini Force had ever been Aries. Ben was about to select the ram symbol, when a wave of regret pulsed through him.

His eyes met Truby's. The man nodded, encouragingly. Ben stepped aside and into the position that had been his mother's – Taurus. He glanced at Truby to see his reaction, but the man's expression was unfathomable.

Addison alone gave him a quiet smile as if to say, *Taurus it is, then*.

Before Ben could think much more into his decision, James began the briefing. He repeated what he'd told them before, but this time with animated graphics of the Nomzamo mine, its three lift shafts, stacked one on top of the other, each one as tall as *three* Sky-High Hotels.

The 'reef' was the narrow seam of gold-rich ore that ran on a diagonal through the earth's crust. It started from a lake that had once been drained to allow digging of the original tunnels. The oldest parts of the mine were only a few hundred metres deep. But as the reef became depleted, they had to follow it down, deeper and deeper. Networks of tunnels existed at each level, each one like a separate unit, connected to other networks via smaller lifts.

The three major lift shafts operated like transatlantic flights connecting continents – mining carriages transporting over a hundred miners to each network of tunnels. Within each network were shorter, narrower bridging lifts. The tunnels at the lowest levels of the mine – where most of the miners were trapped – were already death traps. An ice-making plant on the surface mixed vast quantities of crushed ice with salt and pumped it down to the cooling station underground. Then powerful wind turbines sent ice-cooled air around the mine. Only this made life of any kind possible underground.

'These miners have to be rescued quickly,' James told them. 'That's so long as nothing goes wrong with the cooling plant. If it does, they're already dead.'

He continued, taking questions from the rest of the team. Then began the suggestions. It seemed clear that they'd be taking GF Two, often referred to as *Leo* because its main pilot was Toru.

Ben was itching to fly in *Leo*. He hadn't yet.

James indicated a 3D rendering of an odd-looking craft with wheels and a shiny round cap at one end, about the size of a small tank. 'We're going to use GF Eight. It's a drilling robot. Uses completely new technology, powered by ganymedian.'

'What's ganymedian?' Ben asked.

James looked surprised. He glanced at Truby as if for guidance. Truby nodded. 'He's one of us now.'

One of us.

Ben felt pride and happiness clutch at his chest. He managed to restrain his reaction to a tiny grin.

'Ganymedian, Ben, is something I found on 1036 Ganymed.'

'The asteroid,' breathed Ben. 'So something *did* happen when you went inside that cave you found on 1036 Ganymed?'

Truby conceded a small nod.

'I thought maybe aliens,' Ben admitted.

Truby responded with a bark of laughter. 'This was a lot less scary. But maybe just as exciting.'

'What's ganymedian do?'

'Well, I had no clue,' Truby said. 'But it was making my Geiger counter crazy. A kind of radiation we'd never seen before. I brought back as much as I could carry. The terms of my funding for the mission gave me the exclusive mining rights to anything I found.

Fortunately, Trubycom's chief scientist was less clueless than me.'

'It's an energy source?' Ben asked, his mouth dry.

Truby nodded. He waved a hand airily, indicating the entire base. 'And more. You can thank Professor Gerald Anderson for everything you see here. Him and ganymedian.'

'There's a tiny piece of ganymedian inside the nuclear reactor that powers the drill,' James explained. 'It allows the machine to drill up to five times faster than any other drill. We also have to take equipment to remove the debris, fast. And at least two spare drill heads.'

Ben fell into a pensive silence as he listened to the rest of the plan. He'd been let in on the secret of ganymedian – the power source at the heart of GF One, GF Eight and how many other of Gemini Force's machines? Truby was passing it off as a small matter, but Ben knew perfectly well that it was no such thing. He'd been on GF One for almost three months now and had never heard so much as a peep about ganymedian.

It was a secret, all right. How many others were there?

A uniform. A call sign – Taurus. He'd been right – symbols mattered. Just like that, Ben was on the inside.

— LEO —

'You've seen GF Two before, right?' Jasmine watched Ben stare in quiet awe at the aircraft in the hangar bay. The smile vanished from her face as it struck her that maybe he hadn't.

The sleekness of the aircraft's lines were somewhat muted because of the lack of contrast between the vehicle's light-grey paint job – the colour of a foggy day – and the walls of the hangar. Roughly the size of a Boeing 737 but half its height, the flattened wings and body of GF Two made it look a lot like a stealth fighter with more prominent wings. What appeared to be a row of huge windows along the side were actually inlets for the four jet engines that provided vertical lift.

Ben nodded, moving closer. He touched a hand to the tip of the nearest wing, felt the cool of the lightweight alloy that made up most of the aircraft's outer shell. 'Toru showed me, a bit after I arrived. But I've never flown in her. You know, it's made from a lot of the same composite materials as the Airbus A380?'

'Glass-reinforced fibre metal laminate,' she said, with immense confidence. 'My dad worked on its development.' She gestured at a circular panel tucked just below the nose of the craft. 'But did he show you the vortex cannons?'

'Vortex cannons?'

'They fire a ring of compressed air. It's an experimental tech—'

'A weapon?'

Jasmine shrugged. 'Not exactly. You know Truby, with the pacifism. But it's enough to give a hard kick to anyone that tries to physically attack GF Two. I guess we just have to hope that a 'hard kick' is enough.'

He flashed her an admiring smile while Jasmine handed him the grey bundle she'd been semi-concealing behind her back. 'Truby sent this.'

Ben took the bundle. Lightweight woven Kevlar sprang apart in his hands. A Gemini Force jacket. Handling it almost with reverence, he shook the garment. Every wrinkle dropped out.

'Maybe you should put it on?' Jasmine raised a single finger and tentatively touched it to the base of his throat. 'Looks best zipped up to about *here*.'

He did as she suggested. It felt amazing.

'Better than a tuxedo?' he asked, with a wry grin. He could sense himself blushing. Jasmine was gazing at him so intently. Their eyes met for a second. They both burst into embarrassed laughter.

Jasmine wrinkled her nose. 'Hmm, I'd need to see that.'

Toru was right behind them, so preoccupied that he barely glanced up. 'Benedict in a tux? Now there's an image. But dream on, Jasmine. Even Truby won't wear one of those. Ben, get on board.'

Jasmine raised her eyes to Ben. Silently, he wrapped both arms around her shoulders and drew her to him for a friendly hug. 'I guess this is goodbye, for now.'

'Enjoy your first official mission,' she said, her voice muffled against his jacket.

Toru was checking something on the exterior of the fuel panel, but Ben noticed him glancing away as he and Jasmine separated. A little gruffly, Toru said, 'You shouldn't feel left out this time. Auron pretty much insist we're all there as observers.'

Ben said, 'Why would Truby send a team all the way to South Africa if we're not going to get involved?'

Toru's answer seemed rather too vague. 'We can always learn more by being on site.' He finished checking the outside of Leo and headed for the narrow, squat staircase that led to the interior.

Toru wasn't telling him everything, Ben felt sure. What had been said in the conference room before he'd arrived?

Ben turned back to Jasmine, 'We should say goodbye. I guess you're leaving this evening?'

She gave a sad shrug. 'At eight-fifteen from Cancun.'

'Too bad,' he said, not even trying to hide his disappointment. 'Well, enjoy your official sixteenth. Sounds like a laugh, better than your party here, at least.'

'The party here was *fine*,' she told him, eyes bright. And then abruptly, she stopped talking.

Was Jasmine actually misting up? Ben backed away. As cute as she was right now, she was someone else's girlfriend. 'Give Rigel a hug from me, OK? And some of those cheese rinds he likes so much.'

James Winch arrived as Jasmine was leaving. Paul and Lola turned up a few minutes later. Toru had already run through all his system checks and was finalising the flight plan on the on-board computer.

The floor trembled as the hangar bay began to rise. Even from Ben's seat, which was tucked back behind the shell of windscreen over the cockpit, he saw the moment when mid-morning light became visible over the vehicle known as *Leo*.

The ocean came into view. *Leo* was facing outwards from GF One, in vertical launch position. Ben watched Toru's hands as they moved with grace and efficiency over the controls. At the touch of a button, the windscreen tinted as a polarising filter was activated. Outside was nothing but the deep turquoise of the ocean and above it, a flat, white sky.

The craft began to shudder violently as the thrusters powered up. Eventually, as much as fifty metres above the launch platform on GF One, Toru fired the engines. The plane bolted forward, rapid acceleration evident in the roar of the thrusters.

He felt the crush of G-force pressing him back into his seat, which was behind the co-pilot's. Today, Paul Scott was in that position. *Leo* burst through the uniform layer of cloud, to a glorious blue sky above. Ben was going to fly higher than he ever had – suborbital. Straight up, until the turning of the Earth did most of the travelling for them, and then descent on a hard diagonal.

All the way to South Africa – in just over two hours.

Forty minutes into the journey, Ben left the cockpit, made his way to the cargo bay. James and Lola were there, chatting quietly, strapped into a row of seats opposite today's cargo – GF Eight. James patted the empty seat beside his, while Lola gave him a friendly, if rather cool smile. Ben responded with an awkward nod.

Ben sat down. 'This is the ganymedian-powered drill vehicle?'

'It's adapted from a state-of-the-art mine rotary blast drill,' James told him. 'We swapped out the drill bit, used an experimental alloy, fifty per cent more effective.'

GF Eight was about the size of a minibus, mounted on rugged caterpillar tracks and the long arm of the drill lay horizontally in its resting position, encased in a tube of reinforced steel and connected via a hydraulic arm.

'The real difference comes from the power unit – cuts through rock almost twenty times faster than current tech.'

'That's insane.'

James chuckled and nodded. 'That's why I call GF Eight the *Pulveriser*. Mining companies would kill for this tech. Too bad there's no more ganymedian.'

Through a window, Ben caught a glimpse of a city. It passed in the blink of an eye. *Leo* flew over a ridge of rust-coloured mountains and towards the savannah. The land approached at alarming speed. The aircraft lined up, a runway ahead. When *Leo* touched down, it wasn't too different to the landing of any big commercial airplane. It finally came to a halt outside some plain, blockish buildings made of concrete and corrugated, white roofing. There were a few other aircraft around, he noticed, mainly helicopters painted in the red and yellow livery of Mining Rescue Africa.

Toru opened the main door and lowered the ramp. Ben paused in the entrance. He looked out at the airport. Members of the MRA crew were on the ground, wearing red jumpsuits with yellow flashes on the sleeves.

Every one of them stood absolutely still, agape at the sight of *Leo*.

By contrast, Gemini Force's vehicle livery and uniforms were plain and understated. Matt–grey exteriors for the aircraft, with a few white stripes here and there so that they didn't look too military. The uniforms seemed unremarkable, until you touched the fabric. Made of lightweight Kevlar fibres combined with a touch of lycra to fit with smooth comfort, the fabric itself was water-resistant, but a laminate provided splash protection and lent the garments a pearlescent sheen. Inside the jacket, a zip pocket provided a totally waterproof storage option for small items such as a mobile phone. A single insignia identified the wearer – a red, blue and white Gemini Force badge on the right arm.

Not exactly a disguise, yet subtle enough to let the crew pass unnoticed in most circumstances. Just not today.

The low profile might work with a craft like *Scorpio*, which looked like a fancy helicopter, or *Pisces*, which was usually submerged. But *Leo* was extraordinary. Wherever it went, it would attract stares. This airstrip served only the mine. There was no chance of *Leo* going unnoticed. Ben wondered if Mining Rescue Africa and Auron had agreed not to ask too many questions.

Gemini Force had managed to stay off the media's radar – so far.

He reached into his jacket for his aviator sunglasses. This far into the southern hemisphere, even at six in the evening the sun was still sharp and bright. Briskly, James pushed past him, down the stairs and towards the Land Rover that was approaching.

'*Howzit*, James Winch and friends!' called out the driver, a black African woman dressed in a Mining Rescue Africa jumpsuit. She leaned further out of her window. 'Get in, get in! I'm taking you to the village of Harambe, now.'

Ben followed, with Lola and Paul close behind. Toru didn't emerge, even as the Land Rover began to drive away. Ben guessed he was staying behind to watch the aircraft.

The Land Rover left the rough tarmac of the landing strip and makeshift airport. On a dirt track, it headed across the land; dry yellow scrubland, vegetation that barely clung to the baked red earth below, an occasional acacia tree.

Ahead of them, Ben saw a dust cloud. As they drew closer, he saw at the centre of the cloud was a black Mercedes E-class. The Mercedes skidded violently, sent a wave of dust towards them. When it came to a halt, the black car lay across the entire road.

The Land Rover's driver slammed her foot to the floor. Ben felt the vehicle skating across the hard, compacted powder. It stopped, less than two metres from the Mercedes.

Before anyone in the Land Rover could say anything, doors opened on either side of the Mercedes. Two large white men emerged, heads like peanuts on impossibly broad shoulders. As they approached, strolling in a leisurely manner, the two men slid chunky-looking handguns from holsters at their sides. Both weapons were aimed at the Land Rover.

'Oh, man,' Ben muttered. 'That is *not* ideal.'

— SIG-SAUER —

For the third time since he'd first encountered Gemini Force, Ben found himself wondering: *Why aren't we armed?*

Violence didn't come naturally to Ben. He knew that even thinking about joining the army made some people suspect that he was a violent person. He wasn't – but he did believe in a solid defence.

Jason Truby didn't even seem comfortable with *that*. Whatever had gone down in the First Gulf War with his twin brother, it had broken any ideals that Truby might once have had about the armed forces. That was fine. But here they were again, facing down thugs with guns, with nothing better than a few moves learned from the Israeli Defence Force to protect them from bullets.

Definitely not ideal.

'Out of the car,' yelled one of the pink-faced goons. Both passenger doors were yanked open. Huge hands landed on Ben's and Paul's shoulders as they were dragged out. In the next minute they were both spread-eagled against the bonnet as one of the two men searched them, roughly.

Ben bit down on his lower lip, forced himself to stay still. Out of the corner of his eye he could see that Lola was handled more gently. James was the last one out. He emerged with hands held high, volunteered himself for the pat-down. Finally, all four of them were against the Land Rover; Ben, James, Paul, Lola.

The driver, Ben noticed, had remained perfectly still the entire time, at the wheel. She hadn't made a peep.

'Who the hell are you?' barked the shorter of the two men, his accent strongly Afrikaans. His golden, buzz-cut hair sparkled in the rapidly fading sunlight; a sharp contrast with his sunburned face. The second man was older; with greying, short brown hair. This second guy remained silent and watchful, tilting his assault rifle. Both wore grey slacks and navy blue polo shirts bearing the Auron logo and SECURITY emblazoned in white letters across their backs.

'We're rescue specialists,' began James.

Buzz Cut interrupted. 'We saw your airplane landing. MRA told us you're from something called "Gemini Force"?'

'Is "Force" the word that's got you pointing SIG-Sauers at us?' James asked.

'Never heard of you, *skollie*. We checked up. You don't exist.'

Ben glanced nervously at James Winch. The muzzles of the SIG-Sauers were still aimed squarely at his and Paul's head. Yet James seemed calm, almost affable. 'I can assure you that we do. But we're discreet.'

'What about the kid?' Buzz Cut gestured with his

gun. 'And the girl? Expect me to believe that they're *mining* experts?'

'The kid is a trainee. And my female colleague is a medic.'

'*Ag* no, man, you've no authority to be here.'

'You work for Auron, I assume?' asked James. 'Because MRA invited us to observe.'

Buzz Cut yelled, 'This is private land! You're not welcome here.'

'But we might be able to help,' Ben objected. A sharp glance from James silenced him.

Buzz Cut noticed, gave a nasty smile. 'Your little *trainee* seems a bit dumb.'

'Look, you've seen that we aren't armed. If you want us to go back to the airport, we'll just go,' James said, reasonably.

'Not good enough. The only reason for you to be here is that you're hoping to get some intel on the mine.'

Paul and James exchanged disbelieving stares. 'You think we're *spies*?' Paul said.

Buzz Cut just glowered. 'The price of gold has never been higher. Industrial spies are always trying to find a way into Nomzamo.'

Exasperated, Paul said, 'That's ludicrous.'

Ben could tell that James wished the Australian pilot would keep quiet. He kept his own eyes on James. The chain of command in Gemini Force made the engineer today's leader, at least on the ground. Ben watched James sizing up Buzz Cut and his partner.

How serious were these security guys about using those guns? Was all that heavy muscle from weight training, or did they actually know how to move their bodies fast in a tight spot?

With a deliberate, menacing side-step, Buzz Cut moved until his gun was pointing straight into Ben's face. His partner moved across from Paul to Lola. He gave her a thin smile.

'You,' said Buzz Cut, nodding at Ben. 'And the girl. Step forward.'

'Leave them be,' James hissed. This time there was a note of firm insistence in his voice. He took a step forward himself.

'Stop right there!' Buzz Cut's yell instantly raised the tension. Yet he didn't shift his aim.

Ben was still very much staring down a guy with a SIG-Sauer. He was suddenly aware of the trickle of sweat on the back of his neck.

Buzz Cut seemed strangely nervous – given that he and his pal had the weapons while Ben and the rest of Gemini Force had their backs to the bonnet of a Land Rover.

Why was he acting so jumpy?

James was less than two metres away from the barrel of Buzz Cut's SIG-Sauer. While the two men with guns glued their eyes to James and Paul, Ben risked a glance at the ground. He noticed James shuffling closer, the movement almost imperceptible.

Ben yanked his head up, suddenly realising why.

James was trying to move in on the gun. Any normal person would move away.

Krav maga.

James was going to try to disarm Buzz Cut. Ben tried to catch a glimpse of James's left hand. On the shoulder that was hidden from Ben's view, he could just see the vague movement of James's fingers. He was tapping out a signal to Paul.

Were they preparing to disarm both the Auron men? They'd need to get a lot closer.

Buzz Cut had warned James off. Yet he'd actually invited Ben and Lola to step forward.

They didn't seem as threatening, Ben guessed. But Lola and Ben had been trained by James. Maybe, just maybe, that would be enough of an edge.

Impulsively, he stepped forward. 'We'd better do as they say, Virgo,' he said, using Lola's call sign. He put his hands behind his head to conceal the movement of his fingers. Using both hands, he tapped out the signal for 'disarm'. He couldn't see either James or Lola, who were both slightly behind him now. But Ben guessed that Lola had picked up on the message, because she also stepped forward.

Ben lowered his eyes then, pretending to cringe with fear. He began to lower his hands to his sides, holding out both palms in meek submission. 'Wh . . . what are you going to do to us?'

On the word 'us', Ben sprang into action. His right hand whipped across his body, palm spread wide, slapping the muzzle of the gun, while his head and upper body snapped in the opposite direction, away from the gun. He was dimly aware of movement from James, Paul and Lola. They shifted, a blur.

Shots rang out, bullets firing into the sides of the Land Rover. At the edge of his vision, Ben could see James and Paul. They'd slammed their bodies to the ground, the instant he'd moved.

Ben's fist was now wrapped tightly around the wrist that gripped the semi-automatic pistol. He tried to force it down and to his left. It took a few more seconds before he realised that Lola had also been successful. She too was struggling to wrest the second man's gun to the ground. Another couple of seconds and the two Auron men would have overcome them.

But now James and Paul leaped up, threw themselves into the fray. Within another few seconds they'd punched and kicked the two security guards until the weapons were in their hands.

Shaky and covered in fine red dust, Ben rose to his feet.

Amazing. That *krav maga* thing had actually worked.

'*Nice work*, Taurus, Virgo,' said James, approvingly. 'Fast and smooth.'

With a flourish, he released both magazines from the handguns. He kept his eyes on the two security men. They were rising to their feet, looking somewhat dazed. Ben kneeled to pick up both magazines as James hiked the empty SIG–Sauers over his shoulder, into the grassland, at least thirty metres away.

'Now then,' James said, sternly. 'Listen, *bru* . . .' Ben noticed the thick sarcasm as James used the South African slang for 'mate'. 'We may be discreet, but we don't take kindly to being hassled.' He paused. 'Ben, grab their car keys.'

Ben grinned and sped up to a trot as he reached their Mercedes. A few seconds later he was handing the keys to James.

'We're going to get back in our own ride, if you don't mind,' James said. He dangled the keys. 'Probably going to hang on to these for a bit. And your bullets. You'll get them back when we leave.'

'Who do you work for?' said Buzz Cut. All the force had gone out of his voice. But for the first time, Ben could tell that he really, really wanted to know.

James smirked. 'Well shucks, *bru*. I guess we're just a little shy.'

A few moments later, the two muscle-men for Auron were left in a cloud of dust.

'What's got them so narked?' Ben muttered. 'We're only trying to help.'

James glanced sharply at Ben before he replied. 'Maybe that is *precisely* the problem.'

— HARAMBE —

The village of Harambe was little more than a dusty hamlet at the end of a dirt track. It had been a thirty-minute drive from where they'd been held up by the Auron men. The last fifteen minutes had been cautious driving, more pot-hole than road.

The main street, such as it was, was made up of three stores within a single-storey concrete building, each one open to the road. Ben could smell the bakery from the moment he opened the car door. Next to it was a general store that advertised fizzy drink brands like King Malta and Sparletta on fading metal sandwich boards outside. The third seemed to be a dry-cleaner's that also sold mobile phones.

They left the Land Rover to curious stares from some of the young men who leaned on the wall at the edge of the general store. The driver, once again, didn't leave the car. Ben could imagine how much she preferred the air-conditioned cool of its interior to the wall of heat that hit them the instant they stepped out of the car. Ben removed his jacket immediately, tucking it under one arm. Paul and Lola soon did the same.

James disappeared into the general store. He emerged a moment later, followed by a black African man who carried a stack of three chairs in one hand and a small round table in the other. With friendly greetings to all the Gemini Force crew, he set up the chairs and table. A skinny teenage boy followed with another chair and a tray carrying five cans of Sparletta Iron Brew.

James took one can to the driver, while the team took seats at the table. Ben picked up a can, pulled the tab and tasted the fruity, vanilla fizz inside. It was sickly sweet, yet cold and refreshing.

'What's the plan?' he asked James, as the man sauntered back.

'I'm going to meet with some guys from MRA, later this evening,' James replied. 'Those Auron thugs will find us here, eventually. But until they do, we can find out what's really going on with the rescue.'

'It's awful strange that they're prepared to go to these lengths to keep people out,' Lola said, frowning. 'They've got, what – a hundred men trapped down there?'

'You can understand wanting to keep the media out,' Paul agreed. 'But other rescue agencies? That's insane.'

'Maybe James has a point,' Ben said. '"Gemini *Force*" might sound a bit aggressive.'

James gave Ben a warning glance. 'Watch it. Stick to call signs, even here. You never know who's listening.'

He was right, Ben realised. As he sipped the Iron Brew he could sense the villagers watching them, at a discreet distance. The owner of the general store might have been expecting them, but everyone else seemed understandably curious. Suspicious, even.

'What did you mean,' he said, voice now lowered, 'about Auron not wanting help? Do you think maybe they're hiding something?'

James nodded. 'Could be. Something, or *someone*. Might be an idea to hang here for a bit, see what we can hear.'

'We're just going to mooch?' Ben said.

James swigged from his can, grimacing slightly at the taste. 'Mooch away. I'm not expecting the MRA guy for another half hour.'

Ben looked at Lola, hopefully. 'Fancy a walk?'

'Thanks, Ben.' She smiled slightly but shook her head. 'I'm good right here.'

He rose to his feet, trying not to look disappointed. Lola had been avoiding him, lately. It probably had something to do with the fact that he'd admitted to a couple of people on GF One that he *liked* her. It had been true, once, when he first arrived on the base. But the reality of their difference in ages had finally sunk in. He'd tried flirting with her, and nothing. She'd smile at him with this *indulgent* look. As though he were a sweet but occasionally annoying pet.

It had taken Ben a while to interpret those looks of hers, but when he'd realised, it was kind of deflating. Some guys were only spurred on by what they couldn't have, but Ben wasn't like that. At least, not when it came to girls. It seemed like a huge waste of time and energy. He'd given Lola a fair chance to show some interest, and she hadn't. As far as he was concerned, that was it. He wasn't going to be some kind of adoring puppy dog.

The annoying thing was that Lola was keeping her distance right now, when there was really no need. And it wasn't like he could say; *'Hey Lola, it's fine, I don't fancy you.'*

He'd sound like a right muppet.

'I'll just go for a bit of an explore then, shall I?' Ben said.

James nodded, shading his eyes with one hand. 'Don't get lost.'

Ben laughed to himself as he sloped off, can of Iron Brew in one hand. Lost? There was nowhere to get lost. The village of Harambe was a one-road town, with a few very minor dirt tracks leading off from the main centre. He turned right at the end of the shopping area and began to walk. He passed a collection of single-storey houses, most of them half-built, or half-repaired – it wasn't easy to tell.

Boys in shorts and T-shirts played barefoot football across the front of two houses. From the porch of the largest house, a group of young men watched them, occasionally offering shouts of advice.

He must have looked quite a sight, Ben realised, passing by. A white boy in a grey uniform, nothing to do and nowhere to go. Apart from a casual glance, the African guys ignored him. Ben stopped to watch the game. A couple of times the ball veered towards him, but one of the boys always made an extra special effort to catch up to it before it could get anywhere near Ben.

His attention roved towards the last house in the row. Not much there either. The house didn't look bigger than two rooms. The kitchen area didn't even have a proper roof, just a piece of corrugated iron that covered the stove. A young teenage African girl, dressed in what looked like a sleeveless, black neoprene vest and shorts was trudging up to the door. Ben blinked, stopped moving, stared.

A few seconds later, she noticed him too.

Ben moved closer. The girl had paused at the house's dilapidated porch, a rubber and glass facemask dangling from her fingers. She regarded him with detached interest.

'Hi,' he said. He was near enough to see that the girl had been crying. She didn't reply, looking more miserable by the second.

Ben stepped closer. She wiped her nose with the back of a hand.

'What's wrong?' he said, gently.

'You're from the mine?' she asked, hesitant.

'Me? No.'

She nodded and looked away. Ben didn't sound much like a South African, so he guessed that she believed him. She didn't make another sound, but Ben could see that tears had once again begun to roll down her cheeks.

'Hey! What's wrong?' he repeated.

The girl sighed, once. She wiped her eyes, wearily. 'They're all going to die,' she said. She sounded utterly resigned. 'My brother, all of them.'

'The miners? Come on now, don't give up just yet! The rescue guys will get them out.' Ben had no idea how true this was, but he didn't like to see this girl so despondent.

'They won't rescue my brother,' she said.

'Is he a miner?'

The girl nodded.

'My name's Ben,' he said, offering his hand for her to shake. The girl stared at it for several seconds before lightly touching her palm to his. 'What's your name?' he prompted.

'Zula.'

'Well, Zula, I reckon they're doing everything they can to get your brother out. And his mates, too.'

Zula's answer was steadfast, this time. 'No.' Her chin jutted out slightly, a narrow, pointed chin that emphasised the slender, high cheekbones of her face. She was tall and slim, with very serious-looking, almond-shaped, brown eyes. Yet her face seemed very innocent and young. She must be twelve or thirteen, he guessed.

'My brother and his friends, they will die. All the ghosts will die,' she murmured, barely audible. 'All the *zama-zama*.'

Ben said nothing, held his breath as he watched Zula and wondered at the softly-spoken danger in her words. He struggled to think of anyone he'd met who conveyed such depth of sadness, such hopelessness from behind such youthful eyes.

It was wrong. No child should be forced to live with this kind of worry.

Ben wasn't blind to the misery that kids often suffered, around the world. But it was completely different to see it up close and personal. Something within him seemed to twist and struggle, as though his lungs were being slowly squeezed.

What kind of person would he be if he just stood by and did nothing?

Zula's expression shifted as she watched him watching her. She looked bewildered at his concern. She pushed open the front door to her house and made to go inside, but Ben reached for her arm and stopped her. 'Hey,' he said, gently. 'Let me help.'

The door widened and Zula looked down. Ben did the same, and saw a little girl, a toddler, thinner than he was used to seeing toddlers, but standing firmly enough, gripping on to the door and staring up from beneath long, curly lashes with wide, round eyes the colour of treacle toffee. The little girl, who Ben guessed was about two years old, wore no shoes, only a lime-green sundress. Zula pushed past, picked up the toddler on her way into the house, not bothering to see if Ben followed. After a moment, he did.

The house seemed to consist of just three rooms, one of which, the kitchen, was partially exposed. It looked as though the builders hadn't got round to making that part of the house. The only shelter was provided by a sheet of clear tarpaulin coated with a thick layer of dust. It covered a stove, very old, like something from a black-and-white TV show. The door to the second room was closed. There was also a tiny space that was hidden behind a curtain of bamboo. Ben guessed it was a washroom, from the glimpse he caught of a stand-pipe and an aluminium bucket big enough for an adult to crouch inside.

The toddler made a quiet, whining sound and pushed with both hands at the closed door. Zula reached for the handle and let Ben inside. She turned to face him as he looked around at the bare walls, lined with deep cracks in cheap-looking plasterboard. There were two mattresses on the floor. A young woman in her twenties lay dozing on one of them. A man about the same age lay curled up in a foetal position on the other mattress, both his legs bandaged below the knee. Ben looked in silence at the bloodstains on the bandages. They looked fresh.

The woman immediately stirred to full wakefulness.

'How long you been asleep, lazy woman?' Zula said. 'You promised me you'd watch Siba.'

The woman just pulled the little toddler to her and looked up, her expression bland. It was weird. Zula was furiously telling off a woman who looked ten years older than her. Eventually, the woman replied, 'We were awake all night with Dembe. He was in so much pain. Did you bring food, medicine?'

Zula scowled. 'No. I couldn't bring the gold home.'

The young woman looked shocked. 'But . . . But we need the medicine! My husband will die without it.'

'Your man is not going to die,' Zula said, disdainfully. 'You'll get him what he needs, somehow. But my brother has no one but me. Thabo wasn't so lucky as Dembe – he didn't make it out.'

The young woman didn't seem remotely satisfied. She pushed the little toddler at Zula. 'I looked after your sister for you. You're the one who broke the promise.'

Exasperated, Zula said, 'Kamali! You looked after Siba so that I could get the gold that belongs to all of us!'

Zula's raised voice awakened the young man, Dembe, who groaned loudly, twisting on the mattress until he'd located Kamali. She moved towards him with one last, baleful glance at Zula. Curling up behind him, she soothed Dembe by stroking his head, gently, murmuring words of comfort beneath her breath.

Inside that dimly lit room, Ben watched the villagers. He felt pretty uncomfortable to be included in what seemed like private moments of anguish for all of them.

Zula dropped to her knees and clutched at the toddler, absently stroking her thumbs across the little girl's shoulders. 'Everything be OK, Siba, baby, all right?'

'What happened to Dembe?' Ben crouched low enough to be level with little Siba, like Zula.

'He's been shot,' Zula said, curtly. 'He was with my brother when it happened. Dembe's a *zama-zama*.' Ben had the feeling that she spoke reluctantly now. 'Thabo, too,' she continued. 'They bring gold from inside Nomzamo.'

'They steal it?'

Zula looked at him, finally, eyes flashing with cold anger. 'They take gold that the miners don't dig, from parts of the mine they have forgotten. From old places, tunnels that no one will enter any more. Not even the other *zamas*.'

'Why won't they go there?'

She shrugged and looked down at her little sister, avoiding his eye.

'Listen, I know people who can help,' Ben began. If there were unknown dangers facing Gemini Force inside that mine, he needed to find out so that he could warn the others. He wondered how best to get the information from Zula, because she really didn't seem keen to talk.

'All dark places are scary,' she said, suddenly. 'Some of them worse than others. Some places are . . .'

'What . . . haunted?' Ben suppressed the urge to chuckle.

But she faced him then, with firm resolve. 'Yes. Haunted.'

Now he did laugh, softly. 'Come on.' Ben's response seemed to irritate Zula. He decided to change tack. 'So it's you, your little sister and Thabo. What about your parents?'

Zula closed her eyes, briefly. 'Dead.'

'Oh. I'm sorry. Mine too. We're both orphans.'

She only blinked, impassively, at this, as if to say 'but you're not going to die of hunger without them, are you?'

Nervously, he continued, 'And you, what, you and your brother, you live on what he brings from the mine? From the gold?'

She gave a single, proud nod. 'I help him.'

Ben made a mental note to ask more about her parents when she seemed less reticent. For now, he had to find out as much as he could about what dangers his crew mates might face inside the mine. 'Do you know how to find your brother? You know your way around the mine?'

Zula straightened up, a little stiffly. 'Of course. I'm a *zama*.'

There was a low giggle from Kamali. 'Zula is an errand-girl. Only men can be *zama-zamas*.'

'I'm one of them,' Zula insisted, defiantly. 'I help to keep them alive, don't I?'

'She takes food to the *zamas*, and medicine,' Kamali told Ben, saying it as though it were no big deal. Zula clearly disagreed because she lifted the toddler and plonked her into Ben's arms, then stomped out of the room. He was still recovering from the surprise, wondering how to hold the squirming little girl, when Zula returned. In her hands she held scuba diving equipment – an aluminium breathing cylinder and a face mask.

'I guess that explains your neoprene jacket,' Ben mused. He tried to put Siba down but she reached for the hair above his ear and made a fist, grinning in delight. Ben suppressed a protest and pointed at Zula's facemask. 'Scuba diving, hey? I'm a diver too. I've got my PADI certificate, anyway, the basic one.'

After a moment, Siba released his hair and he put her down, immediately. He edged forward, getting a better look at the breathing cylinder. It looked old; the brushed metal was dented and stained from wear and tear. The pressure gauge showed that the tank was less than a quarter full.

'You've been diving?' He looked at Zula with an expression of wonder. 'Where?'

'There's a lake,' she said. 'When they first made the mine, I mean the old mine, they drained the lake. Now there's water again. I dive to the bottom,' she said, directing each barbed word at Kamali. 'I swim through underground tunnels. I get into the mine and I move around it. Like I was born to it, Kamali. And you just stay at home waiting for your husband to return.'

'*And* babysitting your sister,' Ben pointed out, reasonably. 'Fair's fair.'

'Exactly,' Kamali responded, glaring. Her husband had gone back to sleep. Ben wondered vaguely how much blood the guy had lost. Maybe he was in worse shape than Zula seemed prepared to accept.

Ben took one more look at the gathered group. They all looked drained and despondent. He *had* to do something. 'I can get you medicine.'

Kamali sat up, slowly, staring at him.

He glanced at Zula and nodded. 'For your brother, too.'

'I must return to him soon,' Zula said, with an air of finality. She was studying Ben's face now, as though wondering whether she could trust him. 'Or there will be no more Thabo to save.'

Coaxed into conversation, Zula eventually told Ben the whole story.

'Come back with me,' he pleaded, when she was finished. 'Tell my friends what you just told me.'

Zula trembled slightly at this. Her narrow shoulders moved slowly, the most considered shrug he'd even seen. 'No. I must not be seen with you.'

Ben reasoned with her. 'The guys in the street, they saw me come into the house with you.'

'The neighbours, they might stay quiet. The men in the village, they will not.'

He thought fast. How much could he risk telling this girl? It was really James's decision, not his. But Ben felt certain that James would want to help. Maybe Zula's information had something to do with whatever MRA were planning to reveal to Gemini Force?

He had to risk saying something. 'Look, I meant what I said – my friends might be able to help.'

'Then *you* tell,' she said.

'Zula, it's better from you.'

She looked stubborn. 'No. *You*.'

Ben left her house, was back at the general store with the rest of the crew a few moments later. He noticed the stares of a surly huddle of scruffily-dressed young men, who were sharing cigarettes outside the dry-cleaner/ mobile phone store. This time he stared back, at their faces, at their hands, at any exposed skin he could see. Within seconds, he'd spotted proof of Zula's words. There were *ghosts* in the Nomzamo mine.

'Your MRA mate been in touch yet?' he asked.

James shook his head. They'd moved on to a second round of drinks, this time King Maltas.

Ben took a breath. 'I think I know why we're here.' The instant curiosity of the crew spurred him on. 'I just met a girl. She can't be more than thirteen years old. You know what her job is? She's a runner for the *zama-zamas*.' He paused, watching James for a reaction, but there wasn't one. 'It's Zulu slang – for illegal gold miners. It means something like "try your luck".'

At the mention of 'illegal gold miners', James drew a sharp breath.

Ben continued. 'Take a look at the men round here. Look at their faces, their arms. Some of them look pale, don't they? Almost grey. That's from not seeing the sun for months at a time. They *live* down there. That's why the *zamas* are sometimes called *ghosts*.'

Evenly, James concluded, 'The *zama-zamas* are trapped too.'

Ben nodded, then told them what Zula had told him about her brother and life with the *zamas*.

'No parents?' Lola asked, quietly, as though she knew the answer already.

With feeling, Ben replied, 'They're dead.' In that moment he realised why he so wanted to help Zula. Orphans ought to help each other.

'Zula and Thabo found a way into the mine, via the lake. It's about twenty metres down to the bottom of the lake. There are some flooded tunnels. At some point you reach an airlock. Then you're into the oldest part of the mine.'

Lola asked, 'Is her brother also a kid?'

'Thabo is fifteen. Too young to get into the mine like the other illegal miners.'

Paul said, 'How do they get in?'

Ben turned to him. 'The *zamas* have help on the inside. They pay off some of the security guys, they buy stolen uniforms, they walk into the lift. Just like the real miners. Once they're in, they slip away, to the older parts of the mine. And they stay inside for months.'

'You have to bribe someone to steal from the gold mine?' asked Lola.

'I've heard stories about "ghost" miners,' James said. 'Gold mining companies don't like to admit how much gold is being walked right out of their mines. It's no surprise to me that their own employees are on the take.'

Paul asked, 'Why don't all the "ghost" miners get in via the underwater tunnels?'

'The tunnels are narrow in places. Like, collapsed. Zula's dad was a scuba diver, that's how come she and Thabo know how. Not many other miners can dive.'

James took a long sip of King Malta. 'But tunnels can

be cleared. Scuba diving can be learned. There must be another reason.'

'The airlock door is really heavy. It's stiff,' Ben said. 'Zula told me it takes both her and Thabo to open it, from the outside.'

James didn't seem convinced. 'Nevertheless. Airlocks can be heavy, yes, but with the money these guys make from the stolen gold ore, they could pay someone just to wait on the inside, opening the airlock.'

Ben hesitated. Zula had told him why the miners avoided the flooded areas, but he refused to believe it could be so significant. Yet James had seen straight to the heart of it. Maybe it was true?

'The *zamas* are afraid,' Ben admitted. 'They say that part of the mine is haunted, especially the flooded parts. They live for months underground. Apparently, they've made a whole camp. But to get out via the lake, you have to pass through an area that they won't go near.'

'Superstition?' suggested Paul.

'There's often something behind fears like that,' Lola mused. 'How come Zula and her brother aren't scared?'

'Zula *is* scared,' Ben said. 'She told me she feels like every time she goes back into Nomzamo, she's sure it's the last time and she won't get home. But I guess it's the only way they have of getting money now. The older blokes, they can walk in and out easily, just pay whoever they need to bribe. For Zula and Thabo, it's the *only* way.'

'Brave kids,' James said, shortly.

'James . . .' Ben began. His eyes darted across to the half-dozen young African men nearby. Their smoking circle seemed to be edging closer to their table. Ben lowered his voice almost to a whisper. With obvious reluctance, James, Paul and Lola leaned in.

'Zula told me that *zamas* use a bridging lift to reach the newer parts of the mine.'

James's eyes lit up. 'So there's another way into the mine, apart from the main lift shaft?'

Ben nodded. 'I guess there must be. But only if you're higher than the second shaft. The blockage is below that, isn't it? And the *zama-zama* camp is above the second shaft, in the original part of the mine.'

Frowning, Paul said, 'Then why don't the illegals just walk out?'

'They tried; Zula's brother was in the lift with some other illegals. And as they got out, they were shot! By the security guys, I mean. They were trying to stop the *zamas* escaping.'

Lola drew a slow, shocked breath. It was clear from the quiet, stern glances she exchanged with James and Paul that the threat level of this intervention had just gone through the roof. 'That'd explain why those Auron men were so keen to keep us out. You think they want to trap the *zamas* in the old part of the mine?'

'Right,' said Ben. 'I don't think the security guys know about the underwater route. They *do* know that the *zamas* live in the abandoned bit of Nomzamo. I saw one guy, Dembe, who escaped, made it back. Thabo wasn't so lucky, he's stuck in the mine, badly wounded. Zula needs meds, bandages. Then she's going back for her brother.'

'Are you suggesting we help?' Lola asked. '*Leo* always carries a few scubas, just in case.'

'We'd have to go back to the airport. It doesn't sound like there's enough time. Zula didn't really want to talk to me at all, but she's desperate. She's convinced that Thabo won't be able to swim out of there. He's too badly hurt.'

Ben paused then, remembering how the young teenager had broken down at this point, in utter despair. 'I can help to keep Thabo alive a little longer,' Zula had sobbed, 'but for what reason? To die in the darkness, with the rest of the *zamas*?'

'We can get original maps of the oldest parts of the mine,' James said, confidently. 'The construction company that built Nomzamo was Israeli. They'll have all the blueprints. Jason has the right kind of contacts to get this information.' He took out his mobile phone. 'I'll call him, and Toru.' James paused with a finger on his phone. He squinted at Ben, the sun almost directly in his eyes. 'This is very good work, Ben. Good local intelligence-gathering. Your instincts were spot-on.'

'You think we can save them?'

'We have to. Auron is obviously prepared to do anything to stop the world finding out about the *zama-zamas*. So we're their only hope.'

Ben exhaled, slowly. 'That's why MRA had to get

us involved *on the sly*. Maybe they have maps of the original part of the mine?'

James looked doubtful. 'Auron wouldn't hand over that kind of information – not unless they thought it could get their own miners out. No – the Auron miners are trapped in the newest, deepest part of the mine, almost three kilometres down. MRA have to get that second lift running again, or those guys will be cooked. The illegal miners, on the other hand, if they're in the original mine? That's much nearer to the surface. They could reach the first lift shaft.'

Ben said, 'But the Auron guys are stopping them. So they're trapped.'

'I'm betting we can use the *Pulveriser* to drill down in a couple of days and rescue the *zamas*,' confirmed James. 'If we can get hold of the original maps and find a shallower tunnel spot, maybe less. Maybe even a day.'

With a sigh of happiness, Ben leaned back into his chair. All he needed to do now was get the medicines and bandages to Zula. Then he could pass on the message that Gemini Force were coming to the rescue.

Two hours on South African soil and he'd already made himself indispensable, twice. Good progress as far as earning his place on Gemini Force went, perhaps, but would it be enough to save Thabo?

— AIR LOCK —

James's contact at MRA had persuaded the owner of the general store to find the Gemini Force team a place to stay. It was an empty room in the house of a widow whose three sons were trapped inside the gold mine; one a miner, two of them *zama-zamas*.

Ben had helped to make up the camp beds and shared a simple evening meal of stewed pumpkin, beef and rice. Then James, Paul and Lola had set to a detailed discussion of the rescue plan. From what Ben could tell, it was a mostly machine-operated rescue. James would direct GF Eight, the digger, to drill a hole all the way to the nearest tunnel. Then he'd lower Paul down the shaft in an aluminium capsule. He'd locate the illegal miners' camp. They'd rescue the miners one at a time, hauling them up in the capsule.

Zula had described their position as closely as she was able. Paul would have to find his way, using the blueprints of the original mine.

'The *zamas* have made changes,' Zula had warned Ben. 'Don't expect it to be exactly like your maps. Especially the *forbidden* places.'

Once the *zamas* took over part of the mine, pillars that had been left untouched to support the ceilings were reduced. Stopes in which miners had kneeled with hand-drills, scooping out ore, had been backfilled with rock and concrete, to provide extra structural support.

'The biggest danger down there, apart from the humidity and heat,' James had told the team, 'is the seismic activity. All that drilling, it destabilises the rock, big time. Every day inside a mine that deep, they'll feel shocks. Sometimes they're so big that people in the nearby cities think there's been an earthquake. You get these rock bursts, practically without warning. Shards of rock, flying through the air like they've been shot from a gun. Toxic gases that'll have you passed out in less than five minutes. That's why anyone who goes in there has to carry a Dräger Oxyboks self-rescuer. If the worst happens, at least you'll be able to breathe.'

As James continued to describe the mine and its perils, Ben realised that there was little hope that he'd be allowed to help much with this rescue. His mild claustrophobia wasn't going to be any help to anyone.

Nomzamo was so much worse than a deep, dark hole from which trapped miners needed to be pulled. It was a shifting, shuddering space, a dungeon as deep as two huge skyscrapers were tall. Dark, implacable; a place of tightly-drawn breaths and suffocating heat.

Maybe he'd at least be allowed to learn to operate the drilling vehicle, GF Eight, or the pulley that would wind up the capsule? Even that would take some persuasion.

Mind buzzing from everything he'd seen and heard, Ben slipped away under cover of darkness. The inside of his jacket was warmed by three large pockets of flatbread stuffed with leftovers from their evening meal. At Zula's house, Ben handed out the food to Zula, Kamali and Dembe. He watched as Zula first broke her wrap in two and handed half to Siba. The toddler ate with relish, obviously famished, while Zula and the adults ate with more measured bites, savouring the food.

Then Zula led him out of the main room and into the empty kitchen, moving by the glow from a single candle held inside a used beer bottle. Ben watched her face light up as he handed her the first aid pouch he'd made up from Lola's supplies. 'It's got all the usual, sterile dressings, antiseptic wipes. There's a pain-killing injection too.'

Zula's eyes filled with gratitude.

'Make Thabo as comfortable as you can,' Ben continued. 'My friends and I will come for you both as soon as we can. We're going to drill down into the original tunnels. If Thabo can last for a couple of days, he'll be OK.'

In soft candlelight, her eyes glinted. 'I don't know if he can.'

There was a skittishness about Zula, a kind of restless energy, as if she couldn't wait for him to leave. And when he talked about freeing all the *ghost* miners, she gave him a faint smile, as though the entire topic was a shared joke. As though it were an impossible dream.

Ben looked around for something positive to say. His eyes landed on the diving equipment. 'Don't take any risks down there.' He stopped, unable to continue. Who was Ben to warn Zula of what might happen inside a mine, once systems began to fail? She probably knew the dangers better than him.

She finished off her half of the hot wrap he'd brought. 'I must go now – without Siba seeing, or she will cry.' Zula zipped herself into the neoprene vest and snapped the rubber band of the headlamp over her forehead. Ben watched her spit into the face mask, then rinse it with water from the single tap in the sink.

They were out of the door a moment later, walking across a field from the back of her house, towards a line of trees. Beyond that was the lake.

The sky was potently black, yet filled with brilliant starlight, including, Ben noted, Venus and Jupiter. The two planets cast a very faint glow, enough to see the outline of their path. The surface of the lake appeared slowly as they approached; a glitter of reflected stars. They walked for ten minutes around the edge before she stopped. 'It's here,' she said, pointing. 'Straight down, twenty metres to the first tunnel.'

Ben handed her the nine-litre aluminium breathing cylinder that he'd carried for her. He helped clip it to her back, flicked the pressure gauge, one final check. 'You're running on a quarter of the tank. You sure that's enough? How long will you be down there?'

Zula considered. 'Maybe three minutes. Plus time for the airlock to drain. So yes, I've got enough.'

She switched on the diving headlamp. Rather

abruptly, she hugged him, briefly but tightly. 'Thank you for helping me, Ben.'

He glimpsed Zula's first real smile. Then she was leaping out from the edge of the lake. The sound of her splash was surprisingly quiet. She obviously knew how to enter the water efficiently, slicing down as deep as possible before she flipped over and began to dive. Ben watched the surface of the lake grow still, watched the light from her headlamp disappear. In his mind, he imagined Zula's route.

As James had suggested, blueprints had arrived by email two hours before, sent by the Israeli construction company that had built the original mine. The whole team had studied them on the tablet computers they'd brought along. Ben also had a copy on his own smartphone. He knew that Zula would have to dive almost vertically, until she reached the mouth of the nearest tunnel. It continued at a steep angle, barely walk-able in the days when it was first dug, until it reached the first bend. Then there were two more critical turns before she would reach the airlock.

All that way in the dark. Underground, underwater and alone.

As Ben stood anxiously at the water's edge, a fearful thought struck him. As he focused on it, his fear escalated. He stared at the lake. Hand trembling, he took out his phone, pulled up the map of the mine. His breath seemed trapped and his heartbeat echoed inside his head.

No. He couldn't have been so stupid.

Blinking, he stared in helpless terror at the image on the phone, trying to hold a shaky calculation in his head.

You weren't supposed to make gas tank calculations on the fly. He knew that. You were supposed the check them. Why had he been so quick to trust Zula's own estimate of how much air she had left?

A quarter of a tank – that's what Ben had seen on the pressure gauge. In a nine-litre nitrox tank, at a depth of around twenty metres and possibly under some stress, that was not much more than five and a half minutes. But the map showed that the airlock was at least three minutes away. Plus the airlock-draining time.

She only just had enough air for a one-way trip. Never a good plan. What if something went wrong down there and she needed to bail?

The more that Ben thought about it, the more desperate he became.

The airlock. What had Zula said about it – that she'd always been down there with her brother, because it took both of them to open it from the outside? How was Zula going to open it without help? If she couldn't get in, she'd have to come back. But she didn't have enough air for a return trip.

━ BLOOD GOLD ━

Ben took all of five seconds to make his decision. He reached for his mobile phone, fingers rapidly typing out a message to James Winch.

Zula needs backup or she'll die. And GF could use someone on the inside.

If he asked, the answer would probably be a resounding NO. But if he didn't get down to Zula fast, she'd get too far from where he could reach, just holding his breath. She'd get to the airlock alone. If she couldn't open it, she'd realise too late that she was stuck down there.

A struggle with the door would soak up the last of her air. Then Zula would be in classic diver's no-man's land, with not enough air to get to safety. Thirteen years old and carrying the whole weight of her family on her shoulders. Deep underwater. Trapped, drowning. Just like his mother. Like Caroline.

No. Ben couldn't allow that.

Message sent, he zipped the mobile phone back into the waterproof inside pocket of his Gemini Force jacket. The entire uniform was designed to maintain its shape and fit, in water or out. Everything would dry fast, the minute he was out of the water. Ben took a pen-sized torch from his equipment belt and placed it in his mouth. He set the timer on his watch. He breathed in and out a couple of times, stretching his lungs to their limit. Then he dived, as close to vertically as he could.

Ben could hold his breath for one hundred and ten seconds, on a good day. He was a powerful swimmer, even underwater. But he didn't know the way. If he couldn't find the first tunnel, there were no other options. Zula would be left to *try her luck*. Like a real *zama-zama*.

The water was warm, but stung his eyes, slightly. Ahead, he glimpsed a lip of deeper black in the rock ahead. A tunnel. He kicked harder, angled his head downwards, using arms to pull himself even deeper. The pressure in his ears was mounting. He moved his jaw slightly, allowed the pressure to equalise. But Ben had descended pretty swiftly – more than was advisable. There was now a danger of decompression sickness when he surfaced.

He'd better catch up with Zula – and fast.

His lungs burned. His chest itched and crawled with the effort of holding carbon dioxide in. Every so often, Ben let a few bubbles leak from his mouth. It was a delicate balance – too much and the urge to breathe in became overwhelming. Too little and the burn was too harsh.

If he didn't spot Zula soon, Ben would be forced to turn back. It would be too risky to continue past the point of no-return. He checked his watch.

Fifty seconds gone. One more, powerful kick.

Fifty-three seconds.

A flash of light. The tunnel bent to the right. And Ben could see Zula. She was no more than twenty metres ahead. She moved at a leisurely pace. The kind of pace you set when you feel safe, Ben thought, grimly. He tried to ignore the fire in his chest, the pressure in his head, and swept his arms before him. Five hard strokes. The beam from Ben's flashlight finally reached beyond Zula in the tunnel.

She jerked around, twisting to see behind her. Ben kept swimming. He was desperately close to the last of his air. The urge to gasp was a searing temptation.

Ben swam close enough to see the amazement in her eyes. He just about remembered to ask, before he snatched at Zula's mouthpiece. Since it was the old type, with no secondary demand valve, they'd have to take turns. He released the torch from between his teeth and held a finger to his lips as he mouthed 'air'.

He emptied his lungs, clamped his lips around the mouthpiece and sucked, hard. Sweet, cool air flooded his lungs. It was like breathing the air at the top of a mountain. Almost dizzy with relief, he passed the mouthpiece back to Zula. She was watching him, eyes wide, still shocked by his presence.

Ben put his mouth close to her ear and spoke. His words slurred through the water. 'The airlock,' he said. He checked her eyes, to see if she'd understood. Zula looked confused. After a moment, she nodded. He pointed ahead of them, and mimed the turning of a wheel, then tapped his own chest. Again, she nodded. Ben put a hand to her slim shoulder, gently urging Zula to continue.

They swam together. Every forty seconds or so, Ben would tap Zula's shoulder and they'd stop long enough for him to take a breath.

Sometimes the tunnel narrowed so much that they had to squeeze through in single file. On the second turn, the tunnel began to slope upwards. Ben watched Zula's pace and then slowed it down even further. They were beginning to ascend. It was crucial to do this slowly. Decompression sickness was no joke. Without the proper care, it could leave you brain-damaged or even dead.

Zula appeared to understand why Ben was rising so slowly. *Good*. She'd been taught well. She even sensed exactly when to offer him the mouthpiece.

He could see the airlock now. Bare rock gave way to an enamel-white door, a square metre in the middle of which was a wheeled handle. Ben grabbed it with both hands and tried to turn. It moved, but stiffly. Zula pushed him out of the way. She braced her back to the wall of the tunnel, lodged her feet just below the airlock, where the floor of the tunnel met the wall. Her hands just reached the wheel.

Ben understood immediately. He took up the same position on the opposite side of the tunnel. Hands on the wheel, he began to pull. Zula pushed. The wheel moved slowly but surely, stiff the entire way around, until the very end.

Then the door sprang open. He grabbed the mouthpiece and took a final gasp of the air before waving Zula through. Then he passed through the airlock, and into the sealed chamber, a space that was about two metres across. He closed the door behind them. Zula's hand was already on the lever. When she pulled it down, the water level began to drop. Ben released the last of his own air in a stream of bubbles. As his head emerged from the water, he took a slow, careful breath.

Zula's own head rose out of the water. She pulled off her mask. They were both soaked through, warm lake water dripping into their eyes. Ben allowed himself a relieved grin, wiping his face with the back of his sleeve.

She beamed at him, threw both arms around his waist and pressed her face against his chest, briefly. 'You came to help me.'

'Yeah . . . I decided you were probably being a bit hopeful about that airlock,' he said. Ben was a little taken aback by the enthusiasm of Zula's greeting, but didn't resist. Until an unwelcome thought occurred to him. 'You knew that I'd come after you.'

Zula shook her head. 'No.'

'Yes,' he insisted. 'You're the one who said you couldn't open the airlock on your own. Is that even true? Or did you just say it to make sure I'd follow?'

She shook head again, more vigorously. 'I hoped . . . but I didn't know for certain.'

'Why do you need me, anyway? To find your brother?' he said, puzzled. 'You know your way around here better than me. What good am I?'

She didn't answer for a moment, waiting for the water to completely drain away. Then she was pulling on the second door, the one exit to the chamber. This wheel, Ben also noticed, was too stiff for the girl.

'Good thing I did follow you,' he said, turning the wheel. Zula looked up, sharply. She'd caught the hint of disapproval in his tone.

'My brother may already have bled to death,' she hissed. '*Ben*, Siba and me – we couldn't survive without him. Without . . .' She broke off suddenly. Abruptly, she stepped through the second airlock door.

Ben paused for a second before he followed her out of the chamber. Something wasn't right, here. What was Zula not telling him?

'You can't survive without your brother,' Ben said. He closed the airlock with a brisk turn of the wheel and followed Zula down the tunnel. 'Fine – go find him. You don't need me for that.'

Zula stopped in her tracks. She appeared to be bursting with the desire to say something, angry. 'You . . .' was all she managed to say, as if accusing him.

'What's the problem, Zula? I helped you, all right? And now I'm in trouble.'

'Trouble?' she looked incredulous. 'You saved my life!'

'Yeah, but I left my team,' Ben said, unable to keep a note of resentment out of his voice. Zula had a point. But he was already wondering how to explain this little detour to James and inevitably, Truby.

'I need you,' she blurted. 'You're here now. Help me find Thabo, please.'

'Why?' Ben said, wonderingly. 'You know the way to the camp, I don't.'

She shook her head, trembling slightly. 'No. That's . . . that's not all.'

'Oh. There's something else?'

Zula nodded miserably, raised her eyes slowly to meet his.

'Something you didn't mention?' Ben said, a little harshly.

'Blood gold,' she said, finally. She spoke as though the words even tasted bitter. 'That's what they call what we bring. The gold we take from here isn't pure, Ben. Blood has touched it all.'

'You want me to . . . to help you steal?'

'Our gold is still here,' Zula said, chin raised defiantly. 'The gold that Thabo worked for. I had to hide it, when the mine became a prison.'

'And that's what you came back for,' Ben said, breathing hard as realisation hit him. 'For your *blood gold*.'

Zula refused to meet his eyes.

'I'm here as a *rescuer*, Zula,' Ben declared. 'I'll help you find Thabo, but that's all.'

Between clenched teeth, she said, accusingly, 'You don't think I should be here. You're like Kamali! You think a girl cannot be a *zama*.'

'Absolutely not. It's nothing to do with *that* . . .'

'Kamali!' she repeated, exasperated. 'Happy to just sit back and do nothing.'

'Bit harsh, though. Wasn't she babysitting for you?'

'She – and the others like her, they don't want to read, don't want to learn, they think we should just help the men.'

'Ummm,' Ben said, distinctly uneasy. Was he supposed to agree with Zula? Or with Kamali? 'Maybe that's what Kamali *wants* to do,' he said, tentatively.

'Only because she doesn't know enough. Because she left school . . .'

'Why did she?'

'School costs money. Many parents think it's a waste for a girl.'

Ben said, 'Well, that's a load of rubbish.'

'Yes,' she agreed, passionately. '*Yes*.'

He slowed his pace, taking a moment to look at Zula as she strode with confidence, leading him deeper into the mine. This girl, so intrepid, so determined to find her brother, to keep what was left of her family together – he couldn't help but be inspired.

'Help me to find my brother, Ben,' she pleaded. 'Help me to find our gold. My brother's blood is in that gold. Without it, I will have no home, no food, no school.'

He found himself nodding, slowly. 'All right. I'll do it, Zula. I'll help.'

They were wreathed in clouds of steam. Ben first noticed it when the beam of his flashlight illuminated the halo around Zula. It was thickest around the black neoprene sleeveless jacket that she wore over her swimming shorts.

He became aware of his own misty aura. Inside the heat of the gold mine, water that had soaked into his clothes was vaporising. Ben felt the fabric of his jacket between thumb and forefinger. It was almost dry.

If only his feet were also dry, Ben thought with a touch of shame. Allowing your socks and boots to get soaked through was a survival no-no.

Zula herself wore plastic neoprene shoes with tough rubber soles. They'd dry out as fast as her jacket. After walking about fifty metres, Zula paused at a stope – a narrow niche in the main tunnel. 'Here,' she muttered. 'This is where Thabo and I hide our equipment.' She removed her breathing cylinder and face mask. Then she disappeared for a moment into the gap, emerged carrying two small stainless steel cases and two hard hats equipped with headlamps and clear PVC visors.

Ben took a quick look at the miner's hat she handed him. 'And the gold?' he asked.

Zula lowered her eyes. 'Not here. The *zamas* know we use this place.' She passed him one of the metal cases. 'It's an Oxyboks; a self-rescuer,' she said, as though Ben would know what she meant.

He undid the latch of the Oxyboks case and took a quick look. Inside was a folded, rubber bag connected to a corrugated plastic tube.

'Put the tube in your mouth,' Zula explained. 'The starter cartridge fills the thing with air. Should protect you for around thirty minutes, if we run into poison gas.'

'Thabo's got his with him, right? So why do you still have two sets of kit?'

Zula didn't seem keen to answer, but finally did. 'Thabo wasn't the first *zama* in my family.'

Ben didn't want to know the answer anymore. 'Your dad . . . ?'

She nodded, briefly. Her face was in shadow so Ben

couldn't see if this had upset her. He fastened the hard hat underneath his chin and put the strap of the Oxyboks over his shoulder. 'Good to go,' he said.

They needed to get to Thabo fast.

Ben took his smartphone out of the waterproof inside pocket of his Gemini Force jacket, and pulled up the blueprints of Nomzamo that the Israeli construction company had emailed to Truby. He used his finger to trace a route from the airlock. When he showed Zula, she nodded her agreement and pointed towards the old bridging lift that went down to the newer, deeper sections of the mine.

'What about the *zama* camp?' he asked.

She touched the screen of his phone, dragged the map until they were looking at a network of sloping tunnels. Ben guessed it was at least ten minutes' walk from where they were. 'And the place where you hid your gold?'

Zula shook her head. 'It's not on your map. I told you, there are forbidden areas. Your blueprint, it does not tell the truth about Nomzamo.'

'Well,' Ben said. 'Lead the way.'

The bridging lift was at the bottom of its shaft. Ben was almost afraid that it wouldn't rise when they used the large green button to summon it. The lights didn't work in this part of the mine – why would the electricity supply to the lift work? He didn't have a copy of the electrical engineering blueprints, but Ben guessed that the lift might be on a different circuit.

After a few seconds, they both heard metallic whirring. The lift arrived a moment later. The doors opened. Inside was a cage large enough to fit eight men. Stepping inside, Ben faltered for a second. There were bloodstains all over the floor. He dragged his gaze to the walls, fearing the worst. He was right to worry – blood was smeared across the bars.

'My brother rode down in this lift,' Zula said very simply, her voice calm. 'He was escaping,' she murmured, 'with the other *zama-zamas*. But at the bottom of the shaft, the men from Auron arrived. They shot everybody. Then they sent the lift back up. A lift full of bleeding and dying men. The other *zamas*, the ones who were waiting, they took the bodies, brought them to the camp.'

Ben listened, appalled.

Zula was entirely unmoved. 'Ben. I waited, watching them take the bodies away. I waited a long time, then I rode the lift down.'

He was shocked speechless. She'd gone down there, knowing that a bloodbath had met the last *zamas* to try their luck.

'You . . . you risked your life for the gold?'

Zula's eyes met Ben's, full of sorrow. 'I had to. It wasn't just for the gold. You don't understand – *Thabo wasn't in the lift*. He didn't come back up, Ben. They left my brother for dead down there. Bleeding. *Alone*.'

— EXTRACTION —

'You went down to find your brother?'

Zula nodded. 'Yes. I didn't dare move him, Ben.'

'Has Thabo got your gold ore?'

'No – if he did, they would have stolen it. We always hide it. Even other *zamas* cannot be trusted.'

The thought flashed across Ben's mind that this was *real* desperation. There didn't seem to be any honour among these thieves.

Ben realised that he'd never known what it was to go without, had no real understanding of what it must be like to fear for your future at the most basic level. Yet the reality of what ordinary people were prepared to do for gold was absolutely shocking. Living underground for months at a time, in the dark, food and water smuggled in at immense risk. Risking being shot if they were caught.

It was a kind of madness.

About thirty seconds into their journey, the lift began to slow. Ben steeled himself inside the cage, willing himself to be as calm as Zula. It would be nice to think that she had a good reason not to be afraid, that the Auron men had indeed left the area, satisfied that they'd already seen off any *zamas* crazy enough to try to escape that way.

Zula seemed kind of unpredictable. She was no ordinary thirteen-year-old girl. Ben found himself wondering how long she'd lived like this. She'd probably been a normal kid, not too long ago. Now she was more like a steely-eyed professional.

Above the cage, the steel rope groaned as the lift came to a standstill. The doors didn't open. Ben realised that they were stuck. He pushed a hand between them and began to prise them apart. Then they were facing an empty corridor.

Ben stepped out of the lift shaft. This part of the mine was also in total darkness. A low, persistent howl echoed through the tunnels, as though some distant monster was emitting an enormous, never-ending yawn. Together with the knowledge of the immense depths to which they'd sunk, it felt like being buried alive with ghosts.

He guessed they were now level with the first main lift. Any *zamas* who'd managed to get past the Auron men would have been able to find their way to the main part of Nomzamo, mingle with the official miners and escape via the functioning first main lift shaft.

He felt a surge of resentment, thinking about the sheer spite that was operating in this place. Auron could easily have allowed the *zamas* to escape. Yet they'd forcibly trapped up to a hundred men, from Zula's accounts, with no chance to escape.

What kind of evil scumbags would do that?

The tunnels were slightly wider here, enough to fit three men abreast. It wasn't any warmer, which surprised him slightly. The deeper you went, the hotter the rock became. But maybe the low growl of the air had something to do with it.

'That sound – is that what scares people, makes them think there are ghosts?'

'It's the ventilation system,' she replied. 'I've never seen the ice reservoir, because of the guards, but I think it's somewhere close.'

Ben said nothing, but felt his cheeks prickle with the beginnings of a blush. Ghosts. He hadn't meant to take it seriously, but on the other hand . . . the miners apparently did.

She turned then, with the merest glance over her shoulder to check that Ben was following. 'We're close now,' she said.

No more than thirty metres away, they came to a standstill beside another stope. The moment that Zula ducked her head to enter the cubby hole, Ben heard a faint, pain-filled whimper.

Thabo. He was still alive.

Ben leaned against the side of the stope, staring inside. Thabo, a well-built boy with powerful-looking shoulders and arms, was propped up in a seated position. His legs were stretched out, one trouser leg pale, the other dark. It took Ben a couple of seconds to realise that the darker fabric was entirely soaked through with blood. Then he noticed that the rock beneath Thabo was also drenched with the sticky, dark liquid.

'That's a lot of blood,' he murmured. Zula was

already on her knees beside Thabo. She took scissors from the first aid pouch and began to cut, nimbly, at the blood-soaked trouser leg. She discarded the fabric and held her helmet-lamp steadily above Thabo's thigh as she examined the injury. Then she was cleansing a section of his skin with an antiseptic wipe.

'Ben, can you help keep Thabo still?' she asked. 'I'm going to try to get the bullet.'

He froze. Zula was asking him to hold her brother down. The poor guy seemed half out of it anyway. 'You should make a tourniquet first,' he warned, kneeling beside her in the narrow gap, which was now extremely cramped. 'Lots more blood is going to come out if you touch that bullet.'

Ben wished that he'd asked Gemini Force for something more than basic first aid training. Tying a tourniquet, extracting the bullet and stitching were what this situation called for. And he was letting a young girl take care of it.

'Hold him,' she said, quietly.

He pressed his shoulders against Thabo's, keeping the boy's face turned away from what his sister was doing to his leg. After a second he felt the boy flinch, then his body spasmed in earnest as he groaned, loud and anguished. Ben tried to pin him against the wall without being cruel, but was mightily grateful when the boy stopped moving, gasping with relief.

'OK,' Zula said. Between two bloody tweezers she held up a bullet at least three centimetres long. She smiled through her visor, past Ben, at her brother. 'The rest is easy, Thabo. I'll give you an injection, then we can stitch.'

The pain-killing injection Ben had added to the pack was a general analgesic. It didn't exactly numb the sting of being stitched. But as Zula withdrew the injection, Ben began to see the relief of medication flooding Thabo's pain-wracked body, as the boy visibly relaxed.

As Ben watched Zula stitching together the edges of the gunshot wound, he shook his head in amazement. 'You should be working for us,' he said. 'You're incredible, Zula, you know that? I've never met a kid your age who could do that.'

Zula simply gazed up at him blankly. 'There's nothing special here, Ben. All I know is how to survive. When you have nothing and no one, you learn that.'

'I guess you do.'

She rocked back on her heels, admiring her handiwork. Now that she'd wiped away the worst of the blood, it looked surprisingly neat. She peeled the back from a large, antiseptic patch and applied it to Thabo's leg. Her brother looked so relaxed by the pain medication that he seemed ready to pass out.

The feeling seemed to be contagious – Ben himself slumped against the wall of the tunnel, watching Zula slowly collapsing against her brother's torso, as if falling asleep.

'OK,' Ben managed to say, sinking to his knees.

'We've *got* to get some rest. We've both been on the go all day and it's nearly midnight.'

He barely heard her mumbled reply, 'Just a few minutes, then.'

When he opened his eyes, Ben glanced at his watch. It was almost five in the morning. A hand to Zula's shoulder was all it took to rouse her. She stumbled to her feet. 'Now, once again, Ben, I need your help. Do you mind?'

Ben stood, stooping to slide his hands underneath Thabo's shoulders until he had the boy tightly in his arms. 'Happy to be the brawn,' he said cheerfully, using the power in his thighs to straighten his back slowly as he lifted Thabo's full weight.

Luckily, once he was upright, it seemed that Thabo wasn't entirely comatose. He supported himself enough that his feet were planted firmly. The problem seemed to be with moving. That was going to take a whole lot more motivation.

Ben began to speak encouraging words to the boy whose almost-helpless form he was supporting. 'Come on, mate, you can do it, that's it, one foot, yeah, and another, brilliant, mate, that's perfect, do it again, Thabo, yeah, OK, you've got it now, that's what I'm talking about, go on, keep going.'

They managed to get halfway back to the lift. Then Ben felt the first tremor.

It was a slight thing, the merest shudder of the darkened

tube through which they were making such painstaking progress. They stopped moving. Zula exhaled, shakily. It was the first time he'd heard any such sound from the girl.

She glanced over her shoulder at him. 'No . . .' she whispered. Her eyes were pools of fear. 'We have to go back.'

'What?'

But she didn't wait. In an instant, Zula's arms were under Thabo's, alongside Ben's, and she was dragging them both back the way they'd come. The tunnel trembled violently, as though lightning were rippling through the rock walls.

There was an almighty crack: thunder in the walls.

― ROCK BURST ―

Using every ounce of his strength, Ben helped Zula dragged the injured boy back down the tunnel. As the stope they'd just left finally came into sight, he heard a terrible sound.

The rock burst open. The walls shattered. A spray of rock fragments erupted around them.

He threw himself forward, both arms wrapped protectively around Thabo's head. Dozens of flying rock shards jabbed into his legs and back. He swept a hand across his thighs, anxiously checking to see whether any of them had pierced the fabric. There'd be a nasty wound, if so. His hand came away with nothing worse than a film of dust. The Kevlar fibres in the Gemini Force uniform had protected him.

When the worst of it passed, Ben realised that he'd managed to topple into the stope. Zula was embedded a little further in. Thabo was tucked between them. Ben fumbled to feel a pulse in the boy's neck. It was still there.

The air was filled with the rattle of jagged chunks of rock striking every acoustic surface. A silence followed, sullen and morbid in its intensity. The dust settled.

Cautiously, Ben raised his head. The instant that he

inhaled, he began to cough. His mouth filled with dry powder. The choking got worse. Through streaming tears, he saw that Zula was inflating her self-rescuer. Ben held his breath. Hands trembling with urgency, he did the same. Moments later, they both wore the inflated rubber pouches against their chests, teeth clamped around the mouthpiece of the tube that connected to the supply of clean air. Zula set about inflating and fitting Thabo's. He was scarcely conscious enough to take the mouthpiece between his lips.

Talking was no longer a possibility for any of them. The beam from their flashlights barely penetrated the fine mist of dust that now filled the tunnel. But Zula seemed to know where she was going. Once again, Ben positioned his shoulder beneath Thabo's and began to move him out.

They reached the lift. It was definitely much quieter than before. The howling gale that had echoed through the dark tunnels was gone. Ben stepped into the lift cage with Thabo. Zula pressed the 'up' button.

Please let there still be power . . .

The doors closed, the cage began to ascend. Relieved, they removed the breathing tubes. Ben risked a reassuring smile. The lift had crawled upwards for about ten seconds before he noticed that Zula was counting.

When she reached twenty-three, she punched the emergency stop.

'Stay with my brother, Ben,' she insisted. 'I have to get the gold.'

'It's in the lift shaft?' he said, incredulous.

'There's another tunnel.'

Ben watched, curious but also impressed, as Zula climbed up the sheer surface of the shaft. She was impossibly sure-footed. About a metre above the roof of the lift, she appeared to melt into the wall. He waited, listening.

And waited.

Five minutes had passed without any signal from Zula. Ben checked Thabo's pulse, noted the cold, clammy texture of his hands and feet, the boy's shallow breathing. He checked the dressing over Thabo's wound. Spotted with bloodstains, but the worst of the blood loss was over. The only question now was – how much had the boy lost? Ben could feel his own pulse race as panic began to well up within him.

Being trapped in the lift was the worst part of it. Normally Ben wouldn't let himself get this tense. He'd take action – one way or another – and something would change. Helpless inactivity, uncertainty; these were far harder to bear.

Five more minutes passed. Too long. Something had to have happened to Zula. Ben eased Thabo's head to the floor of the lift. He leaped against the cage wall, grabbed the highest point with both hands and pulled himself onto the roof of the cage.

He'd watched Zula climb this wall. Close-up, Ben saw that there were hand and footholds carved into the sheer rock. In another minute he'd climbed up and was inside the other tunnel. This one led deep into the rock, parallel to the one they'd just left.

As he walked, Ben realised that it was another section of the mine. He checked the blueprints on his phone. Nothing he saw corresponded with where he was. Yet the tunnels seemed to mirror the shape and direction of those on the floor they'd just left.

There was no sign of Zula. Methodically, Ben checked each off-branch from the main tunnel, each stope. The floor here was covered in dust and rock shards, but the rock burst seemed to have had less impact than on the level below.

The further he went from the lift shaft, the more Ben began to feel a creeping anxiety. No Zula. He'd left Thabo alone. Surely Zula wouldn't have hidden her gold stash this far from the only exit route?

Tentatively, he called out, 'Zula.'

After a minute even the sound of his own voice was swallowed.

The dark silence that enveloped him began to feel like a tangible thing; cold and empty. Ben felt an involuntary shiver go through him. It was noticeably colder here. The air tasted strange, bitter, like rancid lemons. His heart beat so hard that he could feel his ribs vibrate.

Ben stopped moving, took a deep breath. An image of the hundreds of metres of rock directly above his head popped into his mind. It was almost physically crushing. He visualised, with absolute clarity, another rock burst. This time the tunnels broke, cracked, hunks of rock blocked the exit route. He knew the image wasn't real, but it hooked into his thoughts like a leech. Try as he might, Ben didn't seem to be able to shake it off.

He'd be trapped here, alone. He felt his lungs contract tightly and gasped. Ben fell to his knees, trembling. They were buried. This was a tomb. No one was here. Zula had vanished.

The cold suddenly intensified. A rush of cool air brushed his cheek. Like being kissed by a phantom. Over his entire body, Ben felt his skin crawl. There was a distant yet unmistakeable sound, gurgling, belching. Then far ahead in the tunnel, he heard voices. Men.

They were shocked. They were angry. The voices began to approach, getting louder.

Ben guessed they were no more than a hundred metres away. Beneath the human sounds of fear was another sound, slithering and deadly. It didn't sound like water, but it sounded wet.

He stood, shone his flashlight directly ahead. A slick of darkness was approaching, moving slowly on the ground, much slower than water. It oozed, rather than flowed, like a kind of gel. When the first of it touched his boots, Ben felt the cold. He reached down with the tip of a finger. Freezing slush.

In the tunnel ahead, wild panic. Men were approaching, running for the exit. They were terrified. Then in the midst of all those male voices, a sharp, high-pitched protest.

Zula.

NO HONOUR AMONG THIEVES

Ben willed himself to move. But the sound of Zula's voice up ahead seemed to root his feet deep into the rock. He could hear her struggling, protesting. Whoever these guys were, Zula wasn't their friend.

The tunnel was rapidly filling up with icy slush. It already reached the top of his boots, which had been soaked since he'd dived into the lake. Something must have gone wrong with the cooling system. Ben guessed that it was about another hundred metres to the lift shaft. Every second, the flow seemed to get faster. If he didn't start running soon, the men would catch up with him. He had no idea what would happen then. Would they capture him, as they had Zula? He cast about, urging himself not to panic, trying to assess the fighting space. Wet floors, solid rock walls, the occasional light-fitting. Not much space.

The environment didn't seem to suggest any strategy other than escape.

Yet he couldn't leave Zula to her fate. Ben thought of Thabo, back in the lift. Were the panicked men headed straight there? Ben could feel the muscles in his thighs twitching, desperate to return, to protect the injured boy. But his mind over-rode his instinct. He had to stand his ground and help Zula.

The first miner to reach him hardly even slowed down. He simply pushed Ben out of the way. The hefty shove might have hurt, if not for the fact that at the last second Ben clocked that the running man wasn't going to stop and side-stepped him.

Five more men dressed in rags hurtled past, with barely a glance at Ben, who was now pinned to the side of the tunnel. Then came a group who weren't running, just jogging along. They were led by a wiry black African man about one hundred and seventy centimetres tall, bare-chested and wearing only some very dirty, loose-cut jeans. He was slim, all taut pectorals and sinewy arms.

When he saw Ben his pace slowed. You might even say that he sauntered. The physical confidence of the man was instantly intimidating. Ben edged away from the wall and into the middle, waiting to face the group, standing his ground.

Behind the leader were two other men and in between them, Zula.

The party stopped in front of Ben. Zula said nothing, not a word. Yet her eyes said everything. She was visibly trembling. Ben glanced at her, only to notice that she immediately looked away, avoiding his gaze.

'White boy, what are you doing in my mine?' The group leader folded his arms across his chest and leaned back, looked down his nose at Ben.

'I've come to lead you to rescue,' said Ben, thinking fast. Out of the corner of his eye he saw Zula manage a faint smile.

Maybe she doesn't want them to know we're together?

The bare-chested leader reacted as if caught unawares. It didn't look as though he was used to the experience. He checked a couple of times with the men behind him, as though maybe his own ears and eyes deceived him. Then he reached out with one arm and touched the badge on Ben's jacket. 'You wear a uniform. Who are you?'

'You can call me Taurus. I'm with Gemini Force. We're here to dig out you *zamas*.'

Ben was thinking on his feet here, with the distinct impression that a mistake could have dire consequences. Not just for him but for Thabo and Zula. If anything went wrong, he'd be responsible. And if the rescue of the *zamas* failed because of Ben's recklessness, Truby wouldn't overlook his actions. It was dicey enough when things turned out all right – but if something Ben did actually ended up hurting someone – would Truby forgive that?

The group's leader smiled, a wide, charismatic smile. He held out a friendly hand, shaking Ben's own with a firm, ice-cold grip. 'Taurus of Gemini Force, my name is Richard Mokwene. I thank you for your assistance. Where are the others?'

'Richard, we should keep moving,' said one of the men holding Zula's arm. He flashed Ben a deeply suspicious look.

Richard Mokwene didn't seem remotely moved by his comrade's words. Ben could tell that this was a man used to giving orders. He had an imperious air and Ben guessed that he rarely did as someone else said. For a full five seconds, he faced-down his fellow *zamas*; five seconds in which the only sound was the sloshing of freezing water and ice flowing over their boots. Ben's trousers had only just dried out from the underwater dive, but already they were beginning to soak again.

'Moving, yes,' Mokwene said, eventually. He turned to Ben. 'But where? You, boy.' He poked at Ben's chest. 'You know the way out of here?'

'My friends are drilling an escape shaft into one of the older tunnels.'

'Old Nomzamo?' Richard Mokwene glared at Ben, suddenly wary. He shook his head. 'A bad idea.'

'It's the only way.'

'There are almost a hundred of us,' Mokwene said. 'Many of them won't go near that part of the mine. Bad, bad things happened. The devil lives there.'

'Then you have to persuade them. They'll die if they don't follow.'

A strange smile crept across Mokwene's face. 'There are things worse than death.' He reached back and grabbed Zula by the shoulder, dragging her forward until she was almost nose-to-chest with Ben. 'This one, for example. You heard her shriek? A demon is inside her. Look at her – a child of thirteen years, crawling around inside these tunnels, abandoned by her own father.'

Ben forced his breathing to still, his voice to be even, risked a quick glance at Zula. Unseen by Mokwene now, she mouthed, *Quiet*.

'She's just scared,' Ben said. 'Not mad, not demon-possessed.'

Mokwene laughed. 'White boy, *mlungu*, you know *everything*.' A crafty thought seemed to occur to him just then, and he peered, suddenly suspicious.

Ben's entire body was tense, waiting for the *zama-zama* to speak. The frozen sludge was seeping between his calves now, almost at the knees. Running in this was going to be a nightmare.

'You *know* Zula!' Mokwene said. His eyes widened as he watched Ben try to control his reaction. 'Yes! It's the truth.' He shook Zula's arm, roughly. 'You came to help her.'

'You see this uniform? I'm here to help *everyone*. My friends are drilling down,' Ben insisted, firmly. 'We need to get you all up to the oldest part of the mine. Now.'

'*Mlungu*, I know you lie,' Mokwene said. He shook Zula again by the shoulder, as though she were a rag doll. 'This one came looking for gold. Gold! You see, there is no honour among thieves.'

Zula struggled uselessly in Mokwene's grip. 'I don't need anyone to help me take what's mine.'

The glacial touch of the slush was over Ben's knees now. He began to wonder if they could even make it back to the lift shaft in time. Mokwene shoved Zula aside, thrusting past her towards Ben. Reflexively, Ben took a step backwards, the way James had taught him. It was a cautious movement, the kind that often looked weak.

'The eyes are a good way to determine intent,' James had said. 'But a guy moving into your dynamic sphere – that's always got to be taken as a serious sign that it's about to go off.'

➤ DYNAMIC SPHERE ➤

Mokwene's eyes flickered with curiosity. He stood aside, seemingly considering his next move.

This time, Ben held his ground. His eyes began to take in the area, the distance between himself and the three men, the possible arena for combat. It was theoretically possible to handle three assailants at once. Tim, Paul, Toru and he had tried various exercises.

But a real-life situation, and knee-deep in ice-cold slush? That was a whole other thing. Three assailants wouldn't even fit around him, in the tunnel. That was all to the good, Ben realised. He'd have to take them out, one at a time.

He decided to call Mokwene's bluff. 'Can we please get going? I need you to take me to the *zama* camp.'

Mokwene shrugged and signalled to one of the guys. 'Henry – show Mister Taurus what he needs to see.'

The man who stepped forward with a sly grin was Ben's height; skinny but tough-looking and wiry. He reached for Ben with a lazy, half-hearted lunge, as if to put an arm around his shoulders. Ben flinched, a swift side-step, leaning just out of the attacker's range so that his hand grasped empty air.

Side-step. It's a simple move, but if you really shift, you'll surprise most attackers. Then, it's crucial to follow up – hard.

Ben looped his left hand around the man's outstretched arm, getting a firm grip on his exposed shoulder. Then he held the guy in place while jabbing his right fist into his opponent's kidney.

Three strikes each time, one after another, pow-pow-pow.

The third blow was a hefty shoulder barge, with the full energy of his entire body's momentum. Within three seconds, the *zama* who'd just attacked Ben was falling onto his back, up to his elbows in slush.

Mokwene paused just long enough for Ben to catch the ghost of his grin. Then he launched himself at Ben, who first hopped back onto his right foot, then swivelled to face Mokwene's second attack head-on: a high-energy punch, aimed straight at Ben's eye. He tried to side-step again. Mokwene was too fast. He caught Ben on the side of his head. Pain reverberated behind his eye. If Ben hadn't moved, the blow would have been hard enough to knock him out.

Make no assumptions about your opponent.

Ben blinked, slightly off-balance. He circled away from Mokwene, once again owning his dynamic sphere. He raised both fists to the side of his face, level with his eyes.

Krav maga was supposed to teach you to end a fight quickly, by taking the initiative against an attacker. Ben knew he was in danger of letting the fight come to him. He had to break the pattern.

'Ay!' called Mokwene to his second companion,

beckoning him with a flick of his wrist. The man rushed Ben, both hands outstretched, aiming for his throat. Ben responded fast – a two-handed move. His right palm snapped down over his attacker's left hand, while his left swept the guy's right hand across his own arm. Ben knew he only had the strength to hold him there for an instant, but for one precious second, both Ben's attacker's arms were locked in a cross.

Ben's counter-strike came next; he slammed the heel of his right hand under the *zama*'s chin, jerking his head backwards. The resulting shock to the *zama*'s cervical spine floored him in a second.

Now two men were on their knees in the icy slurry, dazed, recovering slowly. Mokwene's self-satisfied air had vanished. To Ben's horror, he noticed that Mokwene had taken advantage of Ben's distraction to get a tight grip on Zula.

'This *thief* isn't leaving until she shows me where she hid our gold,' Mokwene breathed. He glowered at Ben from beneath his brow.

'Look,' Ben began. He was panting hard, a combination of adrenaline and exertion. 'We all need to leave *right now*.'

Mokwene circled fingers around Zula's throat. His eyes were on Ben's as he asked her, 'What's your opinion, Zama-Zula; are you prepared to leave without the pound of gold ore you took from me?'

'Thabo dug out every grain of that ore! He paid the refiners to extract the gold. It belongs to my brother!'

Zula insisted. Her eyes glistened with tears, the sting of injustice.

A powerful wave of rage buzzed through Ben's neurons. He could feel the anger tempting his fists, sensed blood pounding in his ears. The delayed thrill of overcoming two grown men, even if they were exhausted, hungry *zama-zamas*, was now hitting Ben. It only made the temptation worse.

The desire to lash out at Mokwene was extreme. But Ben suspected this guy might just be able to persuade the *zamas* to travel through the place they most feared in the mine, even more than the sweltering labyrinth that lay beyond the third and deepest lift shaft.

There was still time to salvage this situation. The Gemini Force crew on the surface had Ben's text; they knew where he'd gone. They'd be anxious, sure. After all – they had no way of knowing if he'd made it through the underwater tunnels. But if they could just see past the rule-bending they might also see that it was handy Ben had managed to get inside the mine. Gemini Force needed to be talking to the *zamas*. Ben could be their guy on the inside – he could find the *zamas*, bring them to the rescue shaft.

This could still end well. But not if Mokwene and Zula didn't calm down.

'She comes with us,' Ben said firmly. 'Forget the gold. Survival is what matters. Anyone still standing here in two minutes is going to drown.' He held out a tentative hand to Zula, wary of Mokwene's eyes upon him. The other two men had risen sullenly to their feet. Ben sensed a murderous intent in at least one. But it was obvious that they took their orders from Mokwene.

And as usual, the *zama-zama* leader was impassive, reflective, calm. He reached into a back pocket and withdrew a Bowie knife. The blade's edge caught the beam of Ben's headlamp.

'You fight well, *mlungu*. Maybe you even know how to handle a man with a knife.' With casual deliberation, Mokwene touched the tip of his blade to the base of Zula's neck.

'But this steel isn't for you – it's for her. Zula is the one who's stealing from me. She's the one who hid the gold. So, let's make a deal. I'll show you the camp. I'll talk to the men, see if we can get them to enter the dark zone. And Zula comes along, as my guest. When my men have reached safety, this little one returns with me. Until we find the gold, boy. And – no gold, no Zula.'

⚊ GHOST MINE ⚊

It was too late to run – they could only wade. Thigh deep in the frozen slush, the sharp bite of cold flesh soon overtook every other sensation. Ben could feel himself shivering. Behind him trembling from the cold and the knife at her throat, Zula remained uncomplaining and defiant. She was either unhinged, thought Ben, or else, rather magnificent.

There was no sign of the others, who'd rushed past Ben. He didn't ask after them, either. Mokwene and his men followed Ben back to the lift shaft. Nothing was said, but from the raised eyebrows, together with the silent fury in Zula's eyes, Ben had the impression that they hadn't known about her trick of accessing this tunnel via the lift shaft. And she was quietly livid that her secret was out.

The ice-and-water mixture flowed over the edge of the tunnel and down the wall of the shaft. It had soaked the floor of the lift cage, but had mostly dripped down to the level below.

'The miners are going to die soon,' Mokwene said, with absolutely zero emotion. 'If the air isn't cooled, they will begin to pass out from the heat.'

Thabo lay sprawled on the metal floor, still passed out

despite the icy slush seeping into his clothes, still breathing. Mokwene stood in the corner of the lift, holding Zula to him with one arm, a steady hand on his blade. Ben made the lift return to the top and tried to keep his eyes off Zula. He felt utterly helpless to do anything about her situation. Mokwene gave off a dangerous vibe – the kind of man to flip out, unpredictable and probably vicious.

Ben had met a couple of guys like this before. The first time, on a platform supply vessel that had been escaping the burning debris of a deep water oil platform. Then, a couple of days ago, in the rainforest of Cozumel. Deeply committed individuals with no limits. You could almost smell the *fierce*.

Tackling guys like this – alone – was tantamount to suicide. If only Ben could get a message out to the rest of Gemini Force. But with tonnes of rock between his phone and theirs – impossible.

The lift stopped. Mokwene smirked at Ben, indicating the door. 'Lead the way.'

Ben considered using the blueprint map on his smartphone. But it was the single extra edge he had on Mokwene and his men. If he revealed it now, chances were they'd take his phone and dump him the moment he'd shown them where to wait for rescue.

'She led me here,' Ben said, with a nod at Zula. 'I need you to take me to the camp. And your men, they need to help Zula's brother, 'cause he's pretty badly hurt. Then I'll show you how to reach the place where my friends will come.'

They began to walk. 'You'll be the first into the dark zone,' Mokwene said.

Countless twists and turns later, or so it seemed to Ben, they'd arrived at a place where the tunnel suddenly widened. Broken remnants of tracks on the ground indicated that this had once been used by underground vehicles to transport the ore. He sensed, immediately, that it *had* to be packed with living, human bodies. It reeked of stale sweat, and other even nastier odours were present too, floating underneath the overall rankness.

There were latrines somewhere close by.

'Brothers,' Mokwene called. His voice was firm yet surprisingly tender, as though he was speaking to children. 'Time to leave.'

He heard murmurs, the sound of slow wakefulness as some of the illegal miners were disturbed from their dozing. Mokwene's flashlight suddenly exposed a tunnel lined with hammocks, each strung from empty light fittings. In the shadows they looked like squirming cocoons the size of adult men. One by one, the cocoons spilled their contents and the men began to approach. Ben caught some of their expressions in the beams of his own headlamp. They looked sombre, yet trusting.

'There is a way to escape,' he told them. 'But it is through the dark zone.'

The murmuring instantly became a clamour. In the shifting lights, Ben could see the whites of men's eyes. It wasn't panic, not quite, but a low, mounting dread. Individual voices began to protest.

Ben shook his head in despair. 'You don't have time for this,' he broke in. 'The cooling system has broken down. You must follow me, or you're going to die of dehydration.'

And given the amount of blood he'd lost, Thabo might die even sooner.

As Mokwene began speaking to the *zamas* in a soothing, lilting voice, Ben edged away, trying to look at his smartphone without being seen. He jammed it against the edge of the inflated self-rescuer that still rested on his belly, and risked a swift glance, long enough to see that they needed to pass through the *zama* camp. He turned off his phone.

'It's this way,' he said. He didn't stop to see whether they followed.

'Hey, *mlungu*,' called Mokwene. 'Drop the helmet and the Oxyboks. There are others who need them more than you.'

Scowling, Ben unhooked the inflated self-rescuer, unfastened the helmet and placed both on the ground. 'Any of you want to get out of here alive, come with me,' he said, with as much finality as he could muster.

Minutes later, he'd opened a respectable distance between himself and the illegal miners. The camp had taken minutes to walk through – a long, stinking hive of humanity. He wandered alone, aware of faint mutterings from the group, now more than a hundred metres behind. The only other sound was the occasional squelching noise made by his sodden socks within boots.

He could feel an unnameable sensation rising from somewhere low in his abdomen. Not fear exactly, but close.

Ridiculous, he told himself. This part of the mine couldn't be any worse than any other.

Ben stopped to check his phone. At this distance there was no chance that he'd be overlooked. And yet as he peered at the blueprint map, he sensed that someone was in the passageway next to him, gazing at the bright screen. He swung around.

Nothing.

The sound of the *zamas* behind him seemed suddenly fainter, like far-off whispers. If he was very still, it was almost as though he could make out words and phrases.

Died because of you.

Dead because of you.

Couldn't even watch.

Ben blinked. The air around him felt thick and cold, like a swirl of mist at the top of a mountain just before a snowstorm. A shudder shook his entire frame. His hand went to his throat, as if to ward off an invisible hand that gripped him there. He shook his head, took a couple of deep breaths. The air felt as stale as before, but if possible, even thinner. He inhaled again. This time it made him cough.

He put the phone back in his pocket. 'Hurry up!' he called, as loud as he could, as loudly as he needed to fill the air with his own voice, strong and unafraid.

But you are afraid.

Ignoring the insidious thoughts that were slinking across his mind, Ben resumed his brisk pace. The blueprint showed the way ahead – less than two hundred metres before they reached the tunnel into which GF Eight would drill a shaft. He took a couple of turns and paused. Would the *zamas* be able to follow him? Not without some kind of instruction.

Let's Hansel-and-Gretel this up, he thought. Taking waterproof chalk – a mixture of wax and chalk in a stick – from his equipment belt, Ben marked a hand-sized arrow on the wall to indicate that he'd taken a right turn.

Ben.

His eyes jerked upwards. Then he heard it again. This time it sounded like a sigh.

Ben.

The voice was so familiar. He moved forwards, towards the sound.

Ben, help me.

'Zula?' he called, uncertainly.

Please.

Something slammed into Ben then, knocking him to his knees. He could feel the soaked fabric of his trousers clammy against goose-fleshed skin.

They aren't following any more. You're alone.

To Ben's left, something moved; the shadow of a person.

One of the *zamas* must have caught up.

'Who's there?'

He waited for three seconds, four, seven. Nothing but silence and the distant echo of whispers. He resisted the impulse to speak again. To his right he heard, very faintly, the sound of painful breaths being drawn.

I thought of you.

This time, there was no mistaking the voice. It was his mother.

Ben screwed his eyes shut. He swallowed. It was the air. There was something in the air, messing with his mind. There had to be. And yet, still that insistent sound.

You were in my heart at the end. This isn't what I wanted for you, Ben.

Trembling with a sickening mixture of fear and fury, Ben clamped both hands over ears that burned with the cold.

'Shut up shut up shut up!'

⟝ DARK ZONE ⟞

Even breathing was difficult. Ben felt a pressure inside his head, heaviness and noise, whispers and groans. Someone was drowning, someone was burning.

This is how it's going to be. Blood and death. Flesh and bone.

'No.' He gasped, shaking his head within both hands. 'NO!'

He tried to stand upright, peering down the tunnel. It seemed to be a rocky vortex, swirling into a pitch-black void.

'I'm dreaming,' he muttered, through swollen lips. Even to himself, his voice sounded slow, as if he was drunk.

Then how come you're walking, Carrington Junior?

The voice wasn't his mother's any more; it was the snickering voice of Sandwell, his sixth form tutor from Kenton College. Ben staggered on. His hand shook as he pulled out the smartphone once again to examine the map. It slid out of his hands and onto the rough floor of the tunnel. Ben fell to his knees, feeling faint, one hand fumbling for the phone.

Get up, walk, get out of here, Carrington.

And then another voice, same message. *Get out of here, Ben.*

The shadows that streaked past were always just at the corner of his eye. When he flipped around to look, they'd vanished. Yet when they passed him in the dark, he felt their breath against the back of his neck. Ben heard his own voice on the verge of breaking, calling out to Thabo, to Zula, to Mokwene.

'Don't come up here, don't come.' He could feel his mind breaking, heard his breath come in shaky sobs, like a little boy's. 'Fear of the dark,' he mumbled to himself. He was trembling like a leaf. 'It's only fear of the dark.'

No longer certain that his eyes were reliable, Ben shut them tightly. He kept walking. The fingers of his right hand trailed against the wall of the tunnel, his feet followed the steep incline as the floor began to rise. He was climbing up a hill, felt the sharp angle in the stretch of his calves. It went on for what seemed like long minutes, as he slowly dragged himself out of some kind of pit.

About fifty paces up the incline, Ben's thoughts began to clear. His chest moved evenly, falling and rising in a new-found rhythm. Another twenty paces and there was no sound but his own trudging, wet footsteps and the faint rumble of a drill.

A drill. James had said it might take as little as a day to drill through, if they could find a shallow tunnel. Could they already be close?

Ben began to run.

He reached the spot where the sound was loudest and checked his phone, hoping against hope. Was there any chance that they'd drilled through enough rock to open up communications? Could a signal even find its way down, could it burrow along the narrow rescue shaft?

He gazed, transfixed, at the ceiling of the tunnel from where the drilling sound was loudest.

Come on, James!

Ben waited, listening for the sounds of the illegal miners following. But after fifteen minutes it became clear – they weren't coming. The only way to get the other *zamas* here was to return the way he'd come and drag them back with him.

His muscles just wouldn't cooperate.

It didn't make sense. He'd been through things more terrifying than the dark pit from which he'd just risen. His mother's underwater death, viewed through the cold lens of a webcam. The burning hellfire of the deep water oil platform, Horizon Alpha, when it was on the verge of being dragged to the bottom of the ocean.

The devil lives there, Mokwene had said. He'd called it the *dark zone*.

Ben shivered with a newfound appreciation of that phrase. Darkness that absorbed every positive thought and filled the mind with paranoia. It had to be some kind of residual pocket of poisonous gas. If only they all had Oxyboks self-rescuers, then they'd easily be able to stride through the place. There couldn't be a devil, nor ghosts. Hallucination. It *had* to be.

His rational mind was convinced. Yet, Ben couldn't make his body obey.

Standing on the threshold of the steep tunnel, he began to hear the sound of footsteps. There weren't many. Two, maybe three people. After a minute, he saw the beams of their flashlights.

'Mister Taurus,' called Richard Mokwene. He paused to breathe noisily through a tube. 'You survived the dark zone, I see.'

Mokwene came into view, his right arm crooked firmly around Zula's neck, the tip of his Bowie knife still very much at her throat. Next to him was another *zama*, supporting Thabo under his shoulder, sharing the breathing tube of his Oxyboks self-rescuer. When they stopped moving, Thabo fell in a slump and Ben rushed to catch him before he thudded to the ground.

Mokwene released a satisfied sigh. 'There you are, Mister Taurus; my side of the bargain is complete. You see? Richard Mokwene keeps his word. And now you, little one, you must keep your word, too. Take me to the gold.'

Ben interrupted, 'It's just a matter of time before my friends get through the rock. Listen – you can hear them drilling.'

The narrow cavern fell silent at his words, until the rhythmic hum of the drill swam into focus. Ben placed a hand on the surface of the wall. He could feel the tremor now. An idea occurred to him.

'The way the rock burst, before. Does that often happen?'

Solemnly, Mokwene nodded. 'When they drill, they disturb the rock. Gold comes at a price, *mlungu*.'

Ben felt his mouth go dry. 'It could happen again?'

Next time the air turned into a whirlwind of jagged rocks, the corridor might be packed with bodies.

'It can happen,' Mokwene told him softly, 'at any time.'

'We should find some stopes,' Ben said. 'We were safe inside one of those.'

'Good,' Mokwene said approvingly. He tapped a finger to his temple. 'Now you think like a *zama*.' He peered down at Zula, whose scowling features were still caught in a headlock. 'Our young rescuer learns fast.'

Ben flashed his torch at Zula, watching her blink for a second in its beam. It was unthinkable that Mokwene was going to drag her at knife-point, all the way back down to retrieve her brother's gold stash. 'I'm going with you,' he said, abruptly. 'To fetch the gold. Thabo and the others can wait here.'

Mokwene chuckled. 'You don't trust me?'

'She's a kid,' Ben hissed. 'You're holding a *knife* on a child.'

'And you will not permit that?'

Stubbornly, Ben shook his head. 'I won't.'

He held still, casting a critical eye over Mokwene and Zula. James had trained him to disarm an attacker from the position she was in. But it was just so much theory. Zula didn't know how, and she was the one under the blade.

When it came to defending from knife attacks, Ben knew three moves. That still left the blind-fury, multiple frontal stab for which he knew no defence. He'd been taught to respect knives. They were faster, more flexible and in many ways, more dangerous than guns. When someone had a blade to the jugular of someone you cared about, you pretty much became their willing slave.

One way or another, Ben had to get that knife away from Zula's neck. There didn't seem to be any way to do it, except by negotiating.

'Take me hostage,' he said. 'Let Zula go. She'll lead you to the gold.'

'You believe that?' Mokwene laughed then, so did his companion. 'She'll leave you to die and run for her gold, my friend. Anything else is a dream.'

Ben leaned closer. He'd come to help these people. All they could do was bicker over some lousy yellow metal. And yet – he could almost taste Zula's desperation. If she didn't get that gold, everything they'd been through, she and Thabo, would be for nothing.

The thought chilled his blood with anger at the injustice of it, began to channel into his eyes, his wrists and his fists. He stared hard at Mokwene, a fierce, challenging gaze.

For the first second or two, Mokwene seemed startled. Then the sheer nerve of it got through to him. He raised his blade and gave Zula a shove hard enough to send her flying across the tunnel and into the arms of his companion.

'Hold my things,' Mokwene said to the second man. His eyes bored into Ben's.

Ben's tongue felt suddenly thick, swollen and far too dry. He glanced between Mokwene's eyes and the blade.

Three ways to defend from a knife attack. Not counting running away.

— MLUNGU —

'Look, can we just chill a bit?' Ben began. He raised both hands tentatively before him, tried to keep his voice as low-pitched and relaxed as possible. It probably came out a bit tighter than he'd hoped.

The knife in Mokwene's hand looked suddenly five times as likely to strike as it had when it had been angled at Zula's throat. Shifting his blade from hand to hand, Mokwene regarded Ben with a thin, crooked smile.

'What happened to the brave soldier who came to Zama-Zula's rescue?'

James's advice came back to Ben: *An opponent gets chatty? You ignore his words. Keep your focus on the knife.*

Ben didn't reply, but took a couple of steps back, drawing Mokwene away from Zula and Thabo. When Mokwene followed, Ben wasn't sure whether to be pleased or even more scared. His heartbeat was a steady thudding that made him want to exhale in tiny, breathy gasps.

The strike may come out of the blue.

'Not so brave now, little *mlungu*,' Mokwene muttered, almost to himself. Ben risked the tiniest flick of his attention away from the knife hand and back to the man's eyes. There was no more smile; just cold determination. If the tone of Mokwene's voice wasn't enough to put Ben on high alert, that dead-eyed gaze certainly was. He took a slow, deep breath. He let the memory of months of daily training sessions with James Winch flow through his muscles and bones.

Mokwene's hands crossed once again. This time the knife ended up in his left hand.

The attack came from the top left, an arcing strike, violent jabbing movements and a blood-chilling roar. Ben swept his right hand in a blow to Mokwene's wrist, simultaneously taking a step to the left. His left hand snapped across the space between them, lunging at Mokwene's left shoulder. The *zama*'s weight shuddered against Ben's right hand.

The defence was perfectly executed. The knife strike was blocked. Only a little more force and he'd complete the move, twist the *zama*'s arm behind him and begin the final, disarming manoeuvre. But Mokwene's strength was formidable. His shoulder wouldn't yield to Ben's left hand. The knife arm seemed to be frozen, locked in place, the tip of the blade just centimetres from Ben's right eye socket.

The slightest weakness, any second now, and the knife would be buried to its hilt in Ben's skull.

For several seconds they struggled, releasing tight breaths every so often, feet shifting in the dusty ground as muscles strained in opposition. Urgently, Ben searched his memory for suggestions from James as to how to deal with a deadlock like this. His muscles didn't remember anything, so it wouldn't be fully effective.

Both opponents' knees slammed upwards, simultaneously aiming low blows at the groin. Kneecaps clashed hard in the shared space. The shock of the impact juddered right through Ben, left his right knee shaking. Ben dropped his weight suddenly to the left, letting the full power of Mokwene's attack roll them both to the ground. He felt the knife tip crash into the rock floor, less than five centimetres from his jaw. Mokwene braced his fall with his right hand, left shoulder still firmly in Ben's grip, the man's left wrist still in Ben's right hand. But he couldn't quite make Mokwene angle the knife away, or drop it.

A surge of wild fear coursed through Ben, as sharp as acid. He had to come up with something, or this man was going to kill him. Mokwene didn't seem to know much about how to fight, but he was brutally strong. This wrestling for control of the knife couldn't go on much longer. Ben was going to lose, and Mokwene didn't seem remotely forgiving.

In desperation, Ben wrapped his legs around the man's middle and began to shift his weight, using his hips to roll the man underneath him. When Mokwene drew a sudden, panicked breath, Ben realised with a rush of relief that his opponent was close to giving way.

What happened next was utterly confusing, a shattering blow. As Ben finally began to roll upwards, pushing Mokwene down beneath him, the middle of his back exploded with pain as a devastating kick between his shoulder blades knocked the air right out of him.

His hands flew open, vision blurring. He caught a glimpse of the second *zama* behind him. Mokwene immediately sprang free. Ben tried to draw breath. He couldn't. His chest had seized up. Hands went to his own throat, eyes bulging in panic. After a second or two he was able to catch a brief, shallow breath, which he used to yell out, 'Zula! RUN!'

From behind, he heard shouts. Mokwene's head turned rapidly, facing the same way as Ben, just in time to see Zula disappearing down the corridor. Then Ben was on his knees, trembling and gasping with relief as he fell on his hands.

Mokwene's voice was high, rasping and harsh. 'Who told you to let the girl go?'

'Richard,' said the second *zama*, 'the *mlungu* was about to . . .'

'Get after her, *mampara*!'

The man left in bewildered silence, loping away until Mokwene screamed after him, 'Faster, stupid dog!'

Then Mokwene's voice was at Ben's ear, his words dripping with venom. 'Just you and me now . . . boy.'

Ben's breathing was ragged as he turned slowly to face Mokwene. The man's eyes gleamed, pitiless. He grabbed the collar of Ben's jacket in a fist, dragged him to his feet and threw him hard against the wall of the tunnel.

Never think like a victim. Always attack.

Ben's arms flew behind his back, bracing himself.

Mokwene launched himself into a final attack, his knife held aloft. Ben swung both legs high, connected hard with the *zama*'s chest before the knife could reach him. When Ben's feet landed, Mokwene was reeling, but still upright. He took a second to recover, then lunged once again. This time Ben slipped aside, dipped low as he spun around and arced one leg in a sweeping motion across Mokwene's ankles. When Mokwene stumbled, Ben grabbed the knife hand in his right palm, left hand on Mokwene's shoulder, and applied torsion pressure. This time, it worked. Mokwene's arm yielded, moving backwards until it was impossible for the *zama* to attempt any stabbing motion.

The ceiling above them cracked open.

Dazed for a moment, Ben realised that the background rumble of the drilling had intensified. With the pounding of blood past his eardrums, he hadn't noticed. But now, he sensed a shift in the air. He heard, distinctly, the scrape of metal against rock.

Mokwene jerked away beneath Ben's now-loose hands, shrank back into the shadows.

Ben heard a shuffle. Then silence. He stepped across the tunnel, plucking the torch from its improvised holder in the handrail.

Mokwene was gone.

There was another, deeper ripple of sound from the rock ceiling. Instinctively, Ben shone the light around, looking for Thabo. The boy lay where he'd been left. His eyes were closed. The patch over his wound was soaked with blood. Ben kneeled at his side, feeling deep within the tissue of his neck for a pulse. It was there, but weak.

The entire tunnel began to vibrate as the bulk of the drill began to break through. Ben flopped down next to Thabo, his back to the wall. He wrapped both arms around his knees to steady the trembling. The impact of all that violence was slowly catching up with him, along with his breath.

He could only hope that Zula had managed to get away.

━ METAL COFFIN ━

An aluminium capsule dropped through the ceiling. Ben leaped to his feet just in time to greet Paul as he stepped out of it. The beam of Paul's helmet lamp shone directly in his eyes, but when Ben glanced to one side, he could see that his crewmate was dismayed.

'Where is everyone?'

Ben led him to Thabo, helped the semi-conscious boy to his feet. 'Thabo's been badly shot. You need to put him in the capsule first. Tell James to send down some more self-rescuer kits. There's gas, or something, down there.'

Paul took Thabo's weight and guided him into the open capsule. It was barely wide enough for a person, so there was no need to prop him up inside. He slid a panel across the opening and then touched a switch on the outside. As he and Ben stepped back, the capsule began to rise.

Paul turned to him and Ben thought – *here it comes*.

'What were you thinking, Ben, running off like that?'

Defiant, Ben said, 'I texted James to let you know where I'd gone.'

'D'you at least find the *zama-zama* camp?'

Ben nodded. 'It won't be easy to get them here though. Not without Oxyboks.'

'How many?'

'A handful would do the trick. We could shuttle them back and forth. They're back thataway, through that tunnel,' Ben said, pointing at the map on his phone and then into the shadows that led to the cursed tunnel.

Paul looked thoughtful. 'Poison gas, hey?'

'Or something.'

'We can get the self-rescuers,' Paul said. Then as if it were only now occurring to him, 'What about the girl, the one you followed?'

Ben shrank back, hoping that Paul wouldn't see the colour rise to his cheeks. 'She left . . . .'

'She's got a way out though, hasn't she?'

Ben thought of the underwater tunnel and Thabo's breathing cylinder. He tried not to think about the brutally heavy wheel that opened the airlock. 'There's a way,' he admitted, cautiously. It was too hard to admit that on her own, he really wasn't sure whether Zula could make the trip.

Paul seemed satisfied with the answer. He was in rescue-mode, Ben could tell. Focused and terse, the conversational Aussie banter as distant as the beaches of his native Perth.

'Let's organise this,' Paul said.

And they did. Thirty minutes later, Ben was inside the capsule himself, arms pressed tight against his sides. He took a breath and shut his eyes. Mild claustrophobia was one thing – inside the mine he'd been able to ignore it most of the time, so long as he kept busy. Inside the lozenge-shaped capsule that they were using to shuttle the illegal miners up to the surface, Ben's claustrophobia took on another meaning. His breath hitched a little, he felt an invisible force squeezing him on all sides. In the midst of all that blackness Ben conjured an image behind closed eyelids; the view from the top of the Sky-High Hotel.

No moment in his life had been so open. It was the perfect antidote to the metal coffin into which he'd stepped.

At the time, the scenery hadn't made much of an impression. He'd been focused on the thread of rope that connected him to safety, on the airman they were trying to save, on his mother perched at the summit of the hotel. Now, months later, Ben could recall details of the crowd on the ground below, the solid blue line of the Persian Gulf beyond the beaches, the pale dust of the desert in the distance. He could even smell the sweet notes of burning kerosene mixed into the metallic smoke of the crashed Aermacchi display aeroplane.

Memory. What bizarre things it chose to retain.

The capsule came to a halt. The panel opened and there was James. Like Paul, he looked relieved to see Ben. But also, wary.

Gemini Force had pitched a night-camp beside the drill site. GF Eight stood over the narrow shaft, now adapted to haul the capsule up and down. Lola had her first aid tent set up nearby, a self-contained sterile space. Inside, Thabo was receiving a blood transfusion from Gemini Force's own supply. The hulking shape of GF Two was visible only as a pitch-black silhouette against the star-studded sky.

The *zamas* began to rise steadily to the surface. Ben worked fast alongside James, distributing energy drinks, power bars, bandages and antiseptic wipes for wounds. Within an hour of the first capsule breaking through, they'd rescued twenty *zama-zamas*. Those who were most able began to help with the rescue effort. Ben slipped away for a few moments, to look for Thabo.

The boy was conscious now. He still looked fairly wasted, sitting back in the folding chair, blood streaming from a vinyl bag and into his arm.

'All right, mate?' Ben began, attempting a light smile. But Thabo coughed painfully and eyed him with a cold, hard gaze.

'You left Zula.'

'She left, mate, but I couldn't follow. I went into that hell-hole to rescue you. Not to find gold.'

Thabo shook his head, despondent. 'Why save me, if there's no Zula?' The boy's head was bowed but Ben could hear the sob he gulped down.

'She'll get out,' Ben said, but he could feel his resolve beginning to crumble. 'Your sister is amazing.'

'That is true,' Thabo said, eyes flat, opaque. 'But if he catches her, Mokwene will kill her.'

There was no easy reply.

Between breaths that were increasingly dragged from the surrounding warm air, Thabo said, in a tired voice, 'Talk to me, please. I *hurt*. Take my mind away – tell me a story about you.'

Ben shifted on his haunches, uncertain. 'Like what?'

Thabo's voice softened and his teeth gleamed between parted lips. 'Do you have a girl?'

'Me? No.'

'Aha.' The smile was in Thabo's voice now. 'But you *think* about a girl. Yes?'

'Ummm. Maybe?'

'She likes you?'

'I dunno about that. I made her cry.'

'Ha ha. Yes, she likes you very much, I think.'

Ben wrinkled his nose. 'Somehow, I doubt it.'

'Tell me,' Thabo winced and moved his left leg. 'Why did she cry, your girl?'

'Because she lied to me. I mean, she had to, it was for a thing. She had no choice.'

'Ben! She cried tears for you, because it hurt her to deceive you! Yes indeed, she likes you.'

Thabo's theory and the sudden shift in the tone of their conversation was a bit bewildering. Ben had managed not to think for two whole days about watching Jasmine shed those tears. Put on the spot by Thabo, he was stumbling for a reply, when he heard the raucous sound of heavy wheels on the crumbling dirt track. Fully alerted, he twitched open the flap of the first aid tent and looked outside.

The air was shredded by the sound of a bullet zipping through it less than five metres away from the front of the tent. Ben was about to yell a warning when there was a second shot. And a scream. This time, the bullet took a target.

The camp erupted. *Zamas* who'd been resting, shivering and dishevelled in the cool open air, began to bolt. They scattered randomly as bullets began to fly.

Inside the first aid tent, Ben tipped over the metal stand that held Thabo's blood bag and helped the boy to the floor. 'Stay here,' he whispered, with a glance at Lola, who responded with a firm nod.

Then he was out of the door, running low and fast, in quick bursts between whatever cover he could find. The bullets continued to rain down on the space around which the rescued *zamas* had been clustered. Blood like thunder in his veins, Ben hunted for an escape route.

Tiny orange explosions dotted the landscape between the camp and *Leo*. Incredibly, the guns were all trained on the camp – no one seemed to be firing on *Leo*. It struck Ben that in the darkness, the shooters might not have spotted the aircraft. The dirt track approached from the other side of a rocky outcropping. Gemini Force's largest vehicle was nestled in the crook of that formation.

It looked as though Buzz Cut and his Auron security buddies had finally caught up with Gemini Force and were apparently hell-bent on murdering every *zama* that walked free of Nomzamo.

It was turning into a blood-bath. Just like inside the mine, when a handful of *zamas* had tried to escape into the tunnels that led to the only functional lift shaft.

The difference was, this time, Ben had led them there.

➤ VORTEX CANNON ➤

No one dared move. All motion in and out of the mine had ceased. From his vantage point behind the first aid tent, Ben could see that the body of a *zama* had fallen just in front of the rescue capsule. Another *zama* was crawling on his belly towards his comrade. Shots began to rain down on them, until the would-be rescuer turned and slithered back under cover.

When the gunfire stopped, the air filled with the groans of the injured. The sound of all that agony gripped at Ben's chest. People were injured, maybe dying.

This rescue was turning into a bloodbath.

Their attackers obviously had night-vision technology. They seemed determined to make sure that no survivors escaped. The cruelty of it was astounding. Even if she did manage to outwit Mokwene inside the mine, chances were that Zula would be shot down the moment she emerged.

There had to be something he could do. From where he was, Ben could sneak over to GF Two. As long as the shooters stayed where they were, they wouldn't be able to see the craft, wouldn't be expecting anyone to go in that direction.

There was no way of knowing how much of the area

the shooters had covered. Ben reckoned that within fifty metres, he'd be sheltered by the rocky outcropping. But he'd have to run a gamut at least that long. He rose slowly to his feet, still crouching low.

He took a deep breath, bolted, head down, aiming straight for the hulking shadow of *Leo*. The shots began after two seconds. Blindly, he ran. Bullets zipped past his ears, exploding around his feet. Ben held his breath, kept going. Then the noise was all behind him. He could hear the cars starting up again, driving forwards.

The shooters had worked out that Ben was running *to* something. He'd given away *Leo*'s position. There was no other option now. As he pelted up the landing ramp and into the aircraft, Ben was yelling, urgently, 'Get going! Take her up! Fire the vortex cannons, now!'

Toru didn't need any more persuasion. The engines were already fired up, the thrusters roaring, the ramp closing the second that Ben stepped on board, barely able to strap himself into the nearest seat when he felt the floor shift beneath his feet.

Leo was in the air, flying completely dark as Toru engaged stealth mode. Ben's seat was the nearest to the window; he saw the orange flashes of guns firing upwards, heard the occasional metallic *zing* of bullets ricocheting off the body of the craft.

He felt *Leo* turn in the air. Then they were flying towards the shooters.

'Cover your ears, Ben,' warned Toru. Before Ben could even react, he heard a sharp, high-pitched explosion. It emanated from the front of *Leo*, and whipped through the air. As the aircraft swung around, Ben caught a glimpse of the chaos below. At least one of the shooters' cars was on its side. The gunfire had stopped. He tried to imagine the men on the ground, wondering what the devil had hit them.

A two-hundred-mile-per-hour ring of compressed air. Not exactly a projectile weapon, but it seemed to have stopped the shooting – for now.

There was another tight explosion. This time, Ben felt the kickback as *Leo* shuddered in response. Toru let rip a triumphant cry. Ben didn't join in, an idea had just occurred to him. He began to unstrap himself, gripping the side of the seat as he stood.

'Toru, get me to the lake!' he shouted across the central bay which had previously housed the drilling vehicle, GF Eight. Ben couldn't be sure if Toru had heard him, but a few seconds later the craft was descending vertically. It touched down with a heavy bounce.

Ben didn't waste a second. Less than a minute after *Leo* landed, he was dashing to the equipment closet behind the cockpit. Ben yanked the door open, hunting for the underwater kit.

Toru was beside the door in time to watch Ben scoop up a breathing cylinder, a diving mask and rubber flippers.

'What are you doing?'

'Zula's still down there,' he said, breathless. He clipped the diving tank to his back. 'I can get her out.'

'Dude, you're crazy.'

Ben gave a single nod. 'Probably. But if I don't go and she dies in there . . .' His eyes met Toru's. 'Well, you know how it is.'

Toru conceded the point with barely a blink. 'I didn't bring you here,' he said. He brought his hand down over the button that opened the exit. He watched as Ben readied himself to leave. 'This never happened.'

Ben allowed himself a grin. 'Thanks.'

Then he was out of the door, running straight at the water's edge. By the time he reached it, *Leo* was already in the air. Ben paused, took out his phone, using it to locate the exact place where he and Zula had first entered the lake. Once he'd found it, Ben tucked the phone back into the waterproof pocket. He stepped into the flippers, adjusted the fit, and waded into the lake. When his feet no longer touched the ground, he dived.

The Gemini Force-issue breathing mask was equipped with a headlamp, webcam and underwater microphone. As he carved through the water, Ben clumsily activated all three. He had no idea whether anyone from Gemini Force would be available to watch his progress. But he could hope.

Finding his way back through the underground tunnels was scarier than he'd expected, but at least with flippers, he moved faster. There were more options than Ben had clocked when he'd been blindly following Zula. He lost his way more than once, wound up in dead ends, forced to retrace his strokes in the perfect blackness of the flooded passageways. The sound of his own breathing was almost deafening, a heavy, wheezing sound each time air squeezed through the tubes. He tried to ignore the clatter of his own pulse and heartbeat.

But bloody-minded determination won through in the end. He forced a chill into his own veins by reminding himself of his mother taking her final breaths before the saloon that became her tomb was engulfed with water.

Zula wouldn't die like that. Not on his watch.

The square metal door of the airlock came into view at the end of a tunnel. He swam harder until his hands were on the wheel. Bracing himself against the wall, Ben tugged hard. It moved, but very slowly. Then he felt a sudden release, as though something had unlocked. The wheel ran free for the last half-turn. Ben took his hands off the airlock door for a second and watched as it moved on its own.

Zula was already here. She'd opened it from the inside.

A wave of relief pulsed through him and he blinked as tears of joy sprang to his eyes. He backed off slightly, waiting for Zula to emerge.

She was alive. She'd escaped that hell-hole, gotten out before those psychos had turned up to shoot the illegal miners.

The beginnings of a smile were behind Ben's octopus mouthpiece as the airlock pushed open. The beam from his headlamp caught the first glimpse of hands and then a figure in a diving mask and cylinder. Large hands, strong. Muscular arms that glistened in the watery light.

It wasn't Zula.

Ben froze. He rose slowly to the ceiling of the tunnel, rigid as a sunken branch.

Richard Mokwene.

~ OCTOPUS ~

Mokwene didn't see him. Maybe the light was in his eyes. Maybe he simply couldn't believe what they were showing him. But to Ben's bafflement, the man was twisting in the water from the instant he emerged. As though something was attacking him, from behind.

Then, Ben understood. Mokwene's hands rose to defend his face. One hand stretched out, palm open and grasping. A second later, it was around a slender, delicate neck. And two small hands were grabbing at his mouthpiece.

Zula had been in the airlock too. Mokwene must have gotten in with her, overpowered her and taken her diving kit. He must have held her off as she fought him for the precious air supply, struggling as the water level rose inside the tiny chamber. Then the airlock door must have opened.

She couldn't have much air left. No wonder she was fighting Mokwene. Frantic hands swiped at him, but he held her off with one, unyielding arm.

Ben pushed his feet back against the ceiling, aiming himself at the airlock. He struck Mokwene's back with considerable momentum, felt the man sway, unsteady. Ben didn't pause to let Mokwene pull back a fist. His right hand went straight for Mokwene's face. Ben locked Mokwene in place by sliding his legs around Mokwene's, while he braced a hand up against the ceiling, imprisoning the *zama* against the airlock door.

He felt the man's jaw clamp down around the octopus, refusing to yield it. At some point Mokwene's grip on Zula must have loosened because Ben felt her slide underneath the *zama* leader's arm, until she too was behind him. Air roared in his breathing apparatus as he panted with the effort of holding Mokwene still. Then Zula's hand was on the secondary demand valve of his own scuba set, which was newer and better equipped than the kit that she used when diving. He turned his head slightly to face her, saw her cheeks hollow as urgently, she sucked in air.

Mokwene's struggle became more desperate. Now that he wasn't trying to hold off two of them, his efforts against Ben redoubled. Ben was dimly aware of Zula moving like a shadow in the depths, flitting in and out of his headlamp's beam. Her hands were around Mokwene's waist. The *zama* seemed to register what she was doing. He reached for the girl's head, trying in vain to grab a handful of her hair. Ben snatched at the man's hand with his own. He felt Mokwene straining to turn his body. Bracing his legs even harder against the airlock door, grimly, Ben held on.

Resolve grabbed hold of him and shook him hard.

This was no playful struggle. This was life and death. If Mokwene turned to face him, if he got a hand on Ben's octopus, if he dislodged the hose that connected it to the cylinder, then all was lost. You couldn't win a fight if you couldn't breathe.

Zula's hands began to tug at the breathing cylinder on Mokwene's back. Then Ben understood what she'd done. The girl had unhooked the air tank. Two seconds later she'd disappeared into the darkness, clutching the tank.

Mokwene's entire frame spasmed in panic. With no air, he was out of options.

Ben released him suddenly, sprang backwards. He twisted away from the airlock and began to swim, hard. He clawed at the water before him as he felt one, then two brutally strong hands on his ankles. Frenzied, he kicked at Mokwene's hands, brought the heel of his flipper down, crushingly hard on the man's fingers. He kicked and scraped, felt his foot connect with hands and maybe even a head.

All the while, cold, murderous thoughts flowed through Ben.

You're going to kill him. He's going to drown.

Then as abruptly as Mokwene had gripped him, he let go. Ben shot forwards, didn't stop swimming. He kept going until he was at a safe distance, then stopped.

Heart pounding with a mixture of dread and relief, he turned to look at what he'd done.

The dregs of his headlamp beam reached the door to the airlock as it closed. Ben stared in disbelief. Mokwene hadn't drowned. He'd managed to get back inside. If he could hold on long enough for the airlock to drain of water, he'd survive.

Trapped inside Nomzamo once again, but alive.

Ben couldn't remember how long he hung there, arms and legs outstretched, floating like a starfish in the middle of that sunken tunnel and just breathing. A jolt went through him as he felt a small hand on his thigh. He watched, transfixed, as slowly, Zula emerged out of the darkness to greet him. Her eyes shone with a bright energy. Holding her breath, she smiled. Her teeth caught the rays of his headlamp and her smile was like a crescent moon in a velvet sky. He lowered his gaze to see the breathing cylinder she held loosely between her arms. She raised it to her lips and for a moment, drew breath directly from its nozzle.

He reached out, took the cylinder out of her hands and tucked it underneath one arm. With his free hand, he slipped the octopus from his lips. Bubbles streamed as he mouthed, 'Go back?' pointing one finger upwards.

Zula cracked a wide, excited grin. But as Ben was turning to leave, she grabbed his elbow. He turned back, watching as she reached inside her neoprene vest. Somewhere around her ribs, she pulled out a bulge. It came free, glistening slightly in the beam of Ben's headlamp.

A misshapen grey lump, squashed flat and about the size of a saucer. Within it came the unmistakeable, buttery glint of gold.

GOLD RINGS
AND THINGS

Ben watched, smiling, as Thabo and Zula's hands rested lightly on the inside walls of *Leo*, touching everything just long enough to establish that it was real. Their eyes followed, hungrily taking in everything they saw – from the mundane storage lockers to the control panels in the cockpit. Toru wandered in from outside, where he'd been running maintenance checks on the vortex cannon. He put down his tool box and folded his arms, leaning on a door frame next to Ben.

'This was you, not so long ago,' Toru said quietly, with a quick half-smile at Ben. 'Aww. You were so cute.'

Ben pulled himself up, flushing a bit, still unused to the occasional teasing he got from the pilots of Gemini Force. Toru seemed to detect Ben's instant hostility, and followed up quickly with, 'You got over it, though. Look at you now, you insubordinate little–'

'Yeah, yeah, whatever,' interrupted Ben. 'I appreciate you covering for me. No need to get all parental about it.'

'Parental?' replied Toru smoothly, arching an eyebrow. 'Me? Never. More like a partner-in-crime.

You'd better not tell Truby that I took you to the lake. In fact, you'd better not share details of how Zula got out of the mine, at all.'

'Too late,' Ben grimaced. 'I turned on the camera. GF One must have seen everything.'

'Ah,' Toru said. 'About that. I tuned in for your little show, but I *may* have turned off the feed to the base.'

Ben glanced at Toru in surprise. 'Seriously?'

Toru blinked slowly and smiled.

Ben mouthed a *wow*. 'Nice one.' Then his attention returned to the brother and sister *zama-zamas* who were still wandering *Leo*'s interior.

Thabo took a seat in the passenger area, one hand on his stitches as he winced. Ben crossed the equipment bay, into which GF Eight had been returned, woven metal straps holding it in place.

'You guys are going to be all right,' he said, perching beside Thabo for a quiet word. 'No more being *zamas*, though, 'kay?'

'The gold will get us enough money to last for a year. After that?' Thabo fixed Ben with a conspiratorial look. 'My sister needs to finish school. That costs money. There is no work, Ben, not here. I don't want to move to the city. It is dangerous for kids like us. A lot of crime.'

Ben handed Thabo a business card. 'Jason Truby's contact details. He's fixed you up with a job. With a construction company. The ones who built the mine, actually. You can start when you're feeling better. Just call the guy on this card.'

He followed Thabo's gaze to Zula, who was cheerfully discussing the technicalities of the vortex cannon with Toru. 'You're right about Zula, though. She shouldn't be working. She should be in school.'

'Maybe you should tell her,' Thabo said, with a weak smile. 'She's my younger sister, but many times, it seems like she is the one taking care of me.'

'Me? I can't tell Zula *anything*,' Ben answered, with a wry chuckle. 'Never been any good at getting girls to follow my advice.'

The idea hit him then, something kind of bold and daring, and for a moment all he could do was think about it and wonder if he was brave enough to take the plunge, to say it out loud, to tell her. He stood up and faced her.

'Zula.'

She turned from Toru and gave him a radiant smile.

'You should have your school.' Ben gulped, pushing himself over the final barrier. *Yes.* He could do this. 'You . . . you should have a great school. Free. Until you're eighteen, and then you can go to college.' His eyes gleamed and he felt a burst of warmth within his chest.

'I don't understand,' she said, puzzled.

'There's a house. I inherited it from my mother but . . . I don't need it. The truth is, I don't have the money to fix it up the way it needs. So — I can sell it. I — *we*

– can build a school. And hire teachers and pay them and everything. Then all the kids in your town can go to school. They won't have to be *zamas*.'

Slow comprehension spread across her face. 'Build a school?'

He grinned and nodded, laughing a bit. 'Yeah. Would you like that? I mean, could you see yourself being in charge of something like that?'

Zula blinked. 'Really? Me?'

'I can't think of anyone better. You totally take care of your brother and sister.'

Ben could see her thought processes firing off, furrowing her brow with the beginnings of years of plans. 'I know some men who can build *good* houses,' she mused.

'There you go. That's where you start. Buy land, get builders. Architects to design it.'

'Teachers are more important than bricks,' Zula said.

'True. So find some.'

Her gaze became critical, and a shadow of doubt passed across her face. 'Ben . . . is this real?'

Ben took both her hands and squeezed. 'It will be. Truby will help us with the tricky stuff, I know he will.'

They flew to Sasolburg and touched down briefly on the outskirts of town. Ben said his goodbyes, a matey hug with Thabo and a longer one with Zula. She didn't seem to want to let go. So, a little puzzled, he just let her squeeze him around the middle. Then she raised her head and planted a quick kiss on his cheek.

'Thank you, Ben Carrington. Now I have two brothers.'

'Ha,' Ben said, more than a little embarrassed. 'Anytime, sis.'

He watched them leave GF Two, feeling pride and hope swell his heart.

'That was a cool thing you did, bro,' Toru said, approaching the exit. He paused to watch the siblings walk away. 'That thing about the school.'

Ben smiled. He didn't see the point in hanging on to things he didn't need, not when other people needed them more. 'I'm part of Gemini Force, now. Everything I need is on GF One.'

'It really means a lot to you, doesn't it?' Toru said, eyeing Ben curiously.

With simplicity, Ben replied. 'It's everything.'

Toru grinned and touched a button on the wall panel, closing the exit. 'Then we'd better get you home. Before Denny Atalas takes your spot on the team.'

Ben couldn't stifle a chuckle. 'Ha. Yeah, Denny. Denny's the *man*!'

'He's the dude!'

Now they both laughed. 'Ah well,' Ben reflected, philosophically. 'Nothing's perfect.'

He found himself looking forward to the return journey. They'd stop to pick up James, Paul and Lola, who were clearing up the rescue zone. The *zamas* themselves had taken over site security, patrolling with their own guns to stop any more of Auron's security crew trying to shoot at the escaping *zamas*.

Meanwhile, Auron security had more than enough on their plate as the world's press descended on the main rescue site, from which the hundreds of trapped legal employees inside Nomzamo were beginning to emerge. Mining Rescue Africa had finally succeeded in unblocking the lift and were now starting to haul out the heat-exhausted miners, some of them barely alive.

It made Ben burn with anger to think of how corrupt the whole system was. Security officials bribed to let illegal miners inside Nomzamo, so desperate to hide their own involvement that they'd rather slaughter any potential witnesses to the truth.

Ben sighed and returned to his seat. Why did money have to make everything so complicated? All this hard work, crime and suffering, and for what? An over-priced metal that made everyone go crazy in its wake.

He would *never* buy a girl gold rings and things, he decided. Then his mind began to wander, trying to imagine *which* girl he wouldn't buy gold.

And he realised, with faint surprise, that all those sly digs of Addison's were spot on. It wasn't Lola whose face swam into his mind when he thought of golden gifts.

Now Ben understood why his stomach fluttered a little more than usual when he imagined returning to Gemini Force One. Jasmine had probably already gone back to her mother in Geneva, getting ready to celebrate her sixteenth birthday with her boyfriend and all her school friends. That had been the plan – but on Gemini Force One domestic plans had a way of being put on hold during a rescue mission. Even so, he might be too late to catch her.

But maybe not.

— ACKNOWLEDGEMENTS —

This second instalment of GEMINI FORCE ONE was tentatively positioned as a tsunami story. Jamie Anderson had related a great little anecdote about a time when Gerry had been on holiday at the coast. I was hoping to incorporate it into one crucial scene.

But then I heard a broadcast of a reading from Matthew Hart's book "Gold – Inside the Race for the World's Most Seductive Metal". The sequence in which the author described going into the world's deepest gold mine made the hairs on the back of my neck stand up, made me feel short of breath. A hellish environment, indeed.

My agent, Robert Kirby, had discussed Gerry Anderson's own rationale behind so many THUNDERBIRDS stories – vertigo and claustrophobia were the raw emotions that powered many rescues by INTERNATIONAL RESCUE. A 'mine rescue' story had been one of the future plots suggested by Gerry himself, drawing on his own fascination with a German mine rescue he'd heard on the radio – the broadcast that inspired him to create THUNDERBIRDS.

When a news story broke about illegal gold miners trapped in an old mine shaft, we knew the time was right for this kind of story. It had everything we wanted for GEMINI FORCE ONE – contemporary social justice issues and heavy-duty technology. I began to write GHOST MINE.

Especial thanks to my new editor, Hannah Featherstone, who joined the project at this stage, taking over from Amber Caraveo. Hannah swiftly absorbed the elixir of action, adventure, technology and character drama that hopefully infuses every one of the GF1 stories. She helped me to pack even more punch into the manuscript for GHOST MINE. Meanwhile, Nina Douglas and Fiona Kennedy from Orion Children's Books pulled out all the stops for an impactful launch of book one (BLACK HORIZON), which was happening as we were putting the finishing touches to GHOST MINE.

It's been a ride, writing one book while promoting the previous book in the series, but also terrific fun. Thanks to Rob and Nicole Dyer for their unfailing support for GF1 and its continuation beyond the Kickstarter edition, and to their daughter Addison Nicole for lending us her name. To Andrew Probert for brilliant design work and to Chris Thompson for turning scenes in the book into such amazing art.

Thanks to Jamie Anderson, my new stage-partner, for making all our festival and convention appearances so enjoyable. Thanks to my daughter Lilia for helping out at Hay Festival, and to my husband David and eldest daughter Josie for being the cheerleading team at every

GF1 launch. And as always, thanks to Gerry Anderson, for creating such a brilliant world in which all these characters can have a life.